Once at the Weary Why

by the same author

PEACHTREE ISLAND • SAND IN HER SHOES
THE HOMEMADE YEAR • TALLIE • CRISSY AT THE WHEEL
ONE HUNDRED WHITE HORSES • DREAMBOATS FOR TRUDY
ISLAND SECRET • INDIGO MAGIC • GOOD MORNING, MY HEART
ALONG COMES SPRING • THE QUESTING HEART
THE SHINING MOMENT • FOREVER AND ALWAYS
STARRY ANSWER • GIRL ON WITCHES' HILL
DRUMS IN MY HEART • NO SLIPPER FOR CINDERELLA
THE TREASURE AND THE SONG • REACH FOR THE DREAM
INSIDE THE GATE

Once at the Weary Why

MILDRED LAWRENCE

HARCOURT, BRACE & WORLD, INC.
NEW YORK

All characters in this story are fictitious and bear no relation to any living person.

Once at the Weary Why

One ✢✢✢✢✢✢

"It isn't our world, no, no!
It isn't our thing, yeh, yeh!"

I frowned, and not because of the Florida sun either. "Song
of the Weary Why," blaring across the parking lot in the
Orange Shopping Plaza, was hereby elected my theme song
because this wasn't my world, yeh, yeh, either, not since—
Well, not since a lot of things.

"I see a parking place." I gestured, and Katy Becker,
plumply cheerful, veered around a small parade of cars with
signs saying, *Teachers Care. Do You?* and *Our Children
Deserve Better,* turned sharply left, and stopped with a jolt
against the concrete barrier.

"Actually fifty dollars?" She looked at me as though fifty
dollars were all the wealth of the Rockefellers. "And it isn't
even your birthday!"

"My father is a very generous man," I said loftily.

"Yes, but—" Katy turned to glower at her St. Bernard,
enthroned as usual on the back seat. "No, Brandy, no!"

I couldn't see that Brandy had done anything except sit
there, but maybe Katy was only creating a tactful diversion.

One of the disadvantages of being best friends with somebody as long as I had been with Katy was that she knew as well as I did that until this summer I hadn't even seen my father, much less visited him, since he and Mama got the divorce two years before and that he had never given me fifty dollars all in one chunk before and probably never would again. What Katy didn't know was that the money was a sort of consolation prize for cutting my first visit to New York short so my father and Dina, who was my stepmother but definitely not the motherly type, could go on a cruise with some people who had a boat.

"You're sure you don't mind?" Dina had asked, all smiles and honey now that I was about to leave. "It's business, in a way. We have to keep up our contacts."

So all right. I would have had to come back home to Florida pretty soon anyway on account of school, except— What made me want to sit down and howl like an abandoned puppy was that I didn't feel as though I belonged anywhere any more—not in New York and, worse still, not even here in Valencia, where I had lived most of my life. I reached over to pat Brandy and to get my face rearranged into a semicheerful expression.

"Where first?" Katy asked briskly. "With all that money to spend—"

Brandy whined, but Katy tossed him a Dog Yummie, said, "Stay!" and ran all four windows down a few inches to make sure he got enough air.

"I shouldn't even have brought him," she said, "but he gets lonesome."

I nodded. It wasn't just dogs that felt lonesome or at least out of place.

"What're you going to buy?"

I hadn't even thought about it yet. Maybe I would look

for some dress material or a quart of paint for the fourth wall in my bedroom that I had never finished or the rest of the yarn for the rug I had been hooking for a year or so or even a kit to make one of those tote baskets with *Don't Talk While I'm Interrupting* cross-stitched on it. They were all projects that I had either begun or thought about beginning, like the plaster figurines I had painted when I was in the seventh grade or the scuffs made out of washcloths in the eighth.

"Cammy for Chameleon," my mother had once said when somebody asked what my nickname stood for, "always changeable," but it had been said affectionately, even approvingly, long before Mr. Duncan or Roger or whatever I was supposed to call him appeared on the scene.

When your mother married your school principal (Citrus High School, rah, rah, rah), what *did* you call him? "Mr. Duncan" seemed terribly unfriendly, and "Roger" sounded disrespectful. Mama had been Mrs. Duncan only three months now because she hadn't leaped out and remarried two days after the divorce, the way my father had, and so far I hadn't called my stepfather anything except "you" as in "Will you please pass the butter?" or "Have you finished with the comics?" The truth was that I wasn't exactly used to him yet. Used to him? I didn't know whether I even liked him. All I knew for sure was that our house didn't seem like home any more on account of having one complete stranger in it.

Before, I hadn't felt really desolate about the divorce because I was used to my father's not being home much, anyway, for reasons that there was no sense in hashing over any more. My mother had been there to give me a whole lot of attention, the same as always, so we made a complete family all by ourselves, or so I had supposed. I thought sadly back to our little trips here and there, our chitchat about the Clothes Rack, where Mama used to work, the discussions of the right material for a new dress, the evenings spent trying out different hairdos for me.

It wasn't that Mama dominated me, not that at all, but I had always felt that I was the center of her life, which I certainly wasn't any more. Now it was, "We'll see what plans Roger has," or, "Roger and I are going to a dinner party, so why don't you and Katy get a couple of boxes of fried chicken and eat here?", or just, "I don't have time right now, dear; let's talk about it tomorrow." It just wasn't fair to be the extra person when I had been here first.

The music from the record shop wailed on as Katy and I headed out of the heat into the air conditioning of the enclosed mall.

"Why should we care? Why should we bother?
We're resigning, Mother! It's all yours, Father!"

"Very sound, too," I said. "Did you ever think life's not so great?"

"Oh, I don't know," said Katy. "I'm looking forward to it." She could afford to be cheerful. She had her original parents and no need to fuss around about where she belonged. "Isn't that Jay Vernon over there?"

If she was trying to divert my mind, Jay Vernon wasn't the way to do it. To begin with, I hardly knew him—a teacher's kid, which was two strikes against him. His mother taught music at Citrus, and— Come to think about it, maybe, in a way, I was a teacher's kid now, too, which would be sure to lower my social status, except that I didn't have one. I just kept chugging prosaically along, not especially yearning to be a brain or an activities hound, much less aspiring to go around with Gogi Blakewood and her friends, who were the "in" people at Citrus.

They weren't "in" like cheerleaders or majorettes or football players or members of sixteen clubs. They were "in" by being "out," sort of, so far out that they never bothered to compete. They were just there, with their withdrawn expressions, their shiny cars, and their clothes with all the right labels in them. I knew about labels from prowling through the Clothes Rack—Country Lass dresses, Powder River shoes, Sachs shirts to go with Hammond skirts—very interesting to watch out for in the locker room before gym class.

"Where first?" asked Katy.

Jay Vernon, attired in an old knit shirt, faded blue denim shorts, and sneakers too far gone even for the Goodwill, came striding up, loaded with several disheveled sacks beginning to skid out of control. He plunked them down on the circular seat surrounding the mall's fountain and raised a hand in greeting.

"Shirts, slacks, socks," he said morosely. "My mother has some funny ideas about how I ought to spend my money."

His money? Secure in my own fifty dollars, I lifted a questioning eyebrow.

"Worked for a construction company all summer." Jay flexed his muscles. "Big deal. Hey, did your father go to the meeting? I just dropped Mom off at the stadium, with a carload of banners and stuff."

I frowned. I didn't regard Mr. Duncan as my father, even though he was married to Mama. In fact, I felt as though I were fresh out of parents, with my real father in Dina's sole possession and Mama all starry-eyed over Mr. Duncan—ridiculous, at her age.

"I really don't know whether he went or not," I said.

I dimly remembered Mama and Mr. Duncan muttering about a mass meeting—something about education and the legislature, school things that left me completely uninterested. Jay turned to Katy.

"That big dog of yours. Would you want to rent him out for a walking billboard?"

"Brandy? How did you know I had a dog?"

"Saw you and Cammy out exercising him one day."

"He's over in the car right now, dying to get out," said Katy. "Billboard for what?"

"*Help Our Children by Helping Our Teachers*—stuff like that."

"OK," said Katy. "If you'll walk him, you can borrow him for free. He'll love it."

"Fine! I can trot him around while you're shopping." He hesitated. "I've got to buy some more things myself, though. Mom said today and no later." He dug a grubby list out of his hip pocket. "Would you want to—"

"Oh, sure," said Katy, a very helpful girl. "Cammy can start on it while we go get Brandy." She looked at my doubtful face. "It's in a good cause—help your folks."

I didn't know exactly what the cause was. Besides, I wasn't so much on crusades, especially the kind that adults thought were so terribly urgent. Anyway, the mental image of Jay leading Brandy around with posters attached was just too ridiculous. Probably, though, I should be thankful that he didn't expect me and Katy to take part in the march, too. I held out my hand.

"Give me the list," I said resignedly, hoping there wouldn't be anything on it any more complex than notebook paper. Jay passed over ten dollars, along with the list.

"Just a couple of things she thinks I need." He grinned. "And thanks, chum."

I looked gloomily at the list, written in a stylish backhand that must belong to his mother. "Gym shoes, size 11, at Hanley's," followed by, "Plaid shirt, short sleeves, medium size, at Albin's sale." I wadded up the ten-dollar bill and the list and stuck them into my purse. Just a couple of things! Why didn't his mother stay home from this silly rally and shop for her son herself? On second thought, the teachers were technically on duty this last week before school began —pre-planning, Mr. Duncan called it.

Thinking vengeful thoughts, I darted into Albin's and found exactly the shirt I wanted—a blinding red-and-yellow plaid visible halfway across the store. I smiled smugly. That would teach Jay Vernon not to shove his shopping off on somebody he hardly knew. He hardly knew Katy either, I was sure. Otherwise she would have mentioned it because we had always told each other which boys had spoken to us, which ones we would like to date, and what they said when they did date us—not that we went out a whole lot, and never with anybody as fascinating, for instance, as Eddie Arden, who was one of Gogi's Gang and the absolute living end as far as looks were concerned. Katy and I sometimes consoled ourselves with imaginary conversations in which we grudgingly accepted invitations from an eager Eddie.

"Well, I'm not sure I could go," I would say. "It's rather short notice, but if you wouldn't mind coming a little late, say around nine—" Or, "I have a date for tennis at the Country Club that day." I had never held a racket in my hand. "But I could make it a week from next Friday maybe."

"Revolting!" Katy would say. "Why's he such a big

deal?" Then, giggling, "Because he's good-looking, well-dressed, popular—and doesn't even know we're alive."

I charged into Hanley's—what was taking Katy so long? —and bought the gym shoes, huge clunkers that felt as though they weighed five pounds apiece. Maybe while I waited for Katy, I would stop in at the Clothes Rack for a minute. I wished that Mama still worked there, but Mr. Duncan wanted her to stay home after they got married, so naturally that was what she did. I adored the Clothes Rack's dresses, which had always been too expensive for me, even with Mama's discount. Probably that was where Gogi's Gang bought their clothes, marked with those important labels. Luckily, Mrs. Smart, who owned the shop, was always glad to let me look at dresses that I couldn't afford.

"Here's a little number you could run up on your sewing machine," she would say. "It's the finishing that brings the cost up—fully lined, see, and with the contrasting piping along the front seam."

I paused to stare into the window of the Other Place, which was full of way-out stuff—huge posters of bearded hippies superimposed on blurry scenes of people rioting or throwing rocks at policemen; wall hangings in bright pinks and oranges converging on a swirling center; lamp globes in a dozen colors; gold and silver medallions on heavy chains; pots of huge paper flowers. I hesitated at the door. It would be fun to go in and browse around for a while. After all, I had fifty dollars to spend—not that I was planning to spend any of it here. I walked on and into the Clothes Rack.

"Cammy!" Mrs. Smart rushed forward to greet me. "I was hoping you'd stop by. I have a dress—just came in— that is you, absolutely you!" She gave me a wink and babbled on. "The perfect green for your eyes, and *the* latest thing."

14

I bit my lip to keep from laughing as I played along with her—and not for the first time either. Somebody that Mrs. Smart really wanted to impress must be in one of the fitting rooms with Lulu, Mama's replacement.

"Well," I said, "I hadn't really planned on—"

"Just try it on," Mrs. Smart begged. "I know you'll adore it." She brought out an emerald-green A-line with long gathered-in sleeves and a flat bow of matching suede at the neck. "Hey! I like your new hairdo."

"Why, thank you." I continued to play my role of favored customer. "I just got back from New York."

Let whoever was listening think I had had my hair done in some fashionable salon there. Actually I had copied the hairdo out of the Valencia newspaper—short and almost straight, with bangs, plus a flat curl just in front of each ear —before I even accepted my father's unenthusiastic invitation to visit him and Dina.

"Go ahead," said Mrs. Smart. "Try it on." She nodded her head vigorously to show she meant it.

"All right." If she wanted me to do some free modeling, I didn't mind. "Watch out for Katy going by, will you? I'm supposed to meet her."

As I changed into the green dress, I could hear voices in the next fitting room—somebody young, I thought, maybe buying clothes for school.

"Does this come in hot pink?" a girl asked imperiously. "This shade's not so great on me. And I'll try the turquoise stretch pants and the striped shirt in an eleven."

I gave myself a long look in the mirror. The green dress was, as Mrs. Smart had said, absolutely me. My eyes seemed a deeper green; my skin looked creamier and my hair blacker. Also, to settle any big ideas I might be getting, the price tag said $39.95. It wouldn't be hard to make something more or less like it, though, if I could find the exact same shade of green. I knew Mrs. Smart wouldn't mind, especially if I managed to sell this one for her to whoever was in the fitting room. Lulu, looking harrowed, zipped past me in the corridor.

"Oh, and bring me the ruffled shirt in a nine," another voice called after her, "and the plaid shorts."

I ducked out into the main part of the shop.

"Yes, I know," Mrs. Smart was murmuring to Lulu, "but their folks can afford to buy them anything they like. That kind are hard to suit." She turned to me, raising her voice. "See? I told you! Perfect, absolutely perfect!"

I searched Mrs. Smart's face for a clue as to what I was supposed to do next. In the meantime, I pirouetted in front of the mirror, looking sadly at the dress while Mrs. Smart continued her patter.

"Walk off a little. Just what I thought. You could wear it out of the shop and never have to touch it. Lulu, ask your customers if they want to see this little number while Cammy's making up her mind."

Oh, this was so ridiculous, putting on a great big act just to sell a dress! I had seen that I looked fine in it; I knew that the price was fantastic; I wanted to take it off now and go find Katy.

"Did you decide on something?" Mrs. Smart said as I caught the reflection of a girl coming out of the fitting room area.

"Just looking." The voice was as fretful as I felt. "We don't see quite what we had in mind." It was Gogi Blakewood, with her long blond hair hanging straight and smooth and her blue eyes gleaming under matching eye shadow and thick lashes. I stood staring at her in the mirror. "That's not a bad dress. Do you have it in— Oh, Cammy. Do you work here?"

"No," I said. "I'm trying on a dress."

She shot a glance at the other girl, just coming out of the fitting room with a dress box from Albin's under her arm—Joellen Matthews, who used to be in my English class.

"I didn't know you bought your clothes here," said Gogi.

And I didn't know why she had to act so surprised. My temper flared.

"Oh, it's quite a good shop," I said, not daring to look at Mrs. Smart.

"What's this dress—a Country Lass?"

I smiled faintly.

"You're welcome to look."

She did look, pulling out the label at the back of the neck.

"Oakleigh Hill," she said. "H'm."

H'm to her, too. Even I knew that Oakleigh Hill was to Country Lass as filet mignon was to hamburger.

"I might just take it if you're not going to," she went on.

"Oh, but I *am* going to take it," I said.

"It's $39.95," Mrs. Smart blurted, losing her cool for once.

"That's what I thought." I hauled out two twenty-dollar bills and laid them on the counter. "Oh, and the tax, of course. A dollar twenty?"

Mrs. Smart's face was a study.

"Now, Cammy," she said, "shouldn't you ask your mother?"

"Oh, no," I said airily. "I always do my own shopping. In New York this summer, my father let me buy anything I liked." Anything I liked that didn't cost more than the twenty dollars Mama had given me for spending money. "And go anywhere I pleased, too."

Anywhere to get me out from under their feet in the apartment, I thought bitterly.

"Why don't you go down to the Metropolitan Museum today?" Dina would say brightly. "Or Rockefeller Center? I'd love to go with you, but I just can't today." Or any other day, as it turned out. "I had this luncheon set up ages ago, before I even knew you were coming."

Before Mama wrote and insisted on Daddy's taking me off her hands so she and Mr. Duncan could be alone for a while—or so I surmised. Why else would he invite me when he never had before?

"New York?" asked Gogi. "Down in the Village with the teeny-boppers?"

I evaded her question.

"Rather interesting," I said in a bored voice. "Very—uh—psychedelic."

Gogi seemed to lose interest in New York.

"I heard your mother married Mr. Duncan," she said.

"Yes, she did." I smiled at Mrs. Smart and at Lulu, who was flipping frowningly through the rack of blouses. "Well, see you."

"I know you'll enjoy your dress," Mrs. Smart said mechanically but still with a puzzled expression. "If your mother—I mean, if you want to return it for any reason, feel free."

"Of course," I said, "but I know I'm going to adore it."

Nodding to Gogi and Joellen, I swept out into the mall with my dress box under my arm and sank shakily onto a cast-iron chair beside a palm tree in a huge indoor planter. What on earth had possessed me to spend forty dollars for one dress—a dress that wasn't even on sale? With that money, I could have made myself at least five. I sat scowling at the elegant gold-and-white striped dress box. Of course I knew what had possessed me; I had been determined to impress Gogi Blakewood, who had never given me more than a passing glance before. Probably a passing glance was all she had given me now, but at least she had asked about New York and, I thought, had wanted to buy the dress herself.

But was it really worth forty dollars to exchange a few words with Gogi? Of course it wasn't, but at least I had added a little flurry of excitement to my usual life. I could hardly wait to tell Katy—or would I tell her? On the whole, probably yes, since I would have to explain why I had only $8.85 to spend now instead of $50. As for Mama— Probably Mrs. Smart was on the telephone right now giving her the word. And what would Mr. Duncan think? But I didn't really care what he thought. The money was mine and nobody else's. After all, a senior in high school didn't have to go running to Mama about every little thing, especially under the present circumstances.

"Cammy! Over here!" Katy beckoned from the entrance that opened onto the side parking lot. "Come see Brandy! He makes a great marcher."

Big deal! I could see Brandy any time I wanted to, since Katy and I exercised him every day of our lives, and I didn't see why I should exert myself to go and see how he looked with some kind of silly sign hung on him. Nevertheless, I got reluctantly to my feet and stepped out of the air conditioning into the blazing sun. Grinning, Jay was parading Brandy back and forth in front of the entrance while hurrying shoppers paused to look. From Brandy's collar, decorated with a bright red bow, a miniature cask of brandy dangled, with a hastily scrawled sign, *Revive Our Schools. Write Your Representative.*

"Sorry I was so long," said Katy. "We had an awful time finding the little cask, and then Jay had to make the sign besides, with some crayons from the dime store."

"I'll get Mom to help me make a better one tomorrow," Jay said. "I'm not so great on lettering."

Tomorrow? Was he going to keep this up indefinitely? He

couldn't very much longer, of course, because school would be starting in just a few days.

"I'll be back to get Brandy pretty soon," Katy said vaguely as we hurried back inside. "What's in the box?"

"A dress," I said defiantly, "a new dress that I bought. I—I paid forty dollars for it."

Katy stared, goggle-eyed.

"You did?"

"Yes," I said, "I did."

In a rush of remorse, I was about to add that I wished I hadn't, but before I could utter the words, Gogi and Joellen walked up.

"We're all going to the Weary Why tomorrow night." Gogi addressed herself exclusively to me. After all, she probably didn't even know Katy. "Want to come?"

Since when had the Weary Why changed from a song to a place—and what kind of place? I was smart enough not to ask, though, or to act thrilled either. I answered in what I hoped was a nonchalant voice.

"Well, yes, I guess I probably could."

"I'll send somebody to pick you up around eight," said Gogi, the queen commanding her subjects. "See you, then."

And away she went, leaving me staring unbelievingly after her.

From the record shop a man's voice, laced with the strumming of guitars, sang on,

> "Why should we fight it? Why should we try?
> This is the song of the weary why."

Two ✧✧✧✧✧✧

Out in front, brakes squealed and a car door slammed. I rushed to the window but drew my hand back from the cord of the draw curtains just in time. Maybe it would be bad luck even to look, for fear Gogi's date for me—I hoped it was a date because I didn't want to go to this place, wherever it was, with a bunch of girls—would turn out to be as unthrilling as the dates I got for myself. Anyway, maybe whoever was arriving was only somebody wanting Mama to work on the United Appeal or a man to see Mr. Duncan about his life insurance.

"Cammy." Mama peered into my room. "Your date is here."

I breathed a sigh of relief.

"Is he—" No, I wouldn't even ask because Mama's ideas about a fascinating date wouldn't match mine. "Reliable" would be the key word, which seldom meant "cool." "All right. Thanks."

I wriggled into my new dress and peeled off the Scotch tape that held my two important curls flat against my cheeks.

"You look lovely." Mama gave with one hand and took away with the other. "I'll want you home by twelve-thirty." That was probably a generous hour from her point of view, but I had an idea that twelve-thirty was just the start of the evening with Gogi's Gang. "What's the movie?"

"Nobody said." Why did mothers always think in terms of movies? Maybe the Weary Why actually was a movie, but I doubted it. "Don't wait up, please. I'll be in."

I always did get in on time—with the type of boys I went out with, staying an extra hour or so wasn't especially enticing—and she always did wait up to hear what kind of time I had had. At least she always had until she married Mr. Duncan. Lately she might be awake, but I didn't go into her room any more. I could hardly talk about what I had said and what my date had said with Mr. Duncan in the other bed listening to every word.

I snatched up my purse, took another admiring look at my dress, and hurried Mama down the hall in front of me. For one thing, I didn't want to give her time to comment on my date. She hadn't been much pleased with Gogi's casual arrangements, anyway.

"A blind date? I don't like that."

"But Gogi wouldn't even know anybody absolutely awful," I had protested. "She probably wasn't sure which boy she could get, on account of its being a sudden idea. It might not be a special separate date, anyway. They all run around in sort of a—a swarm. It's just a way of getting there."

Aside from my natural curiosity about who this date might be, another reason for wasting no time arriving in the living room was that I didn't want Mr. Duncan frightening whoever it was with some teacherish remark like "You'll be taking our new World History course this year?" or "Are you going out for track?" I hadn't actually ever heard Mr. Duncan say anything of the sort, but that was no sign that he might not if the notion struck him. After all, what else did principals have to talk about except school? I practically skidded into the room and there, talking to Mr. Duncan, was— I stared unbelievingly. There was probably no law that mirages had to occur in deserts, but I hardly expected one in my living room. I blinked and took a second look. The image snapped sharply into place—not a mirage at all but, miraculously, Eddie Arden.

"Oh, hi!" I looked admiringly at a pale lemon turtleneck shirt, a gold medallion on a heavy chain, lemon slacks barred in red, and blond hair that probably wouldn't look impossibly long to Mr. Duncan, since he was viewing Eddie head-on. Sideways, though, I was pretty sure it was different—not that I thought Eddie was anything but Mr. Terrific himself. "You—uh—know the—uh—family?"

I blamed that inane remark on nervousness. After all, he would know Mr. Duncan at school, and he must have met Mama when he came in. Still, I had to say something.

"Ready?" asked Eddie in a flat voice.

"Oh, yes. Yes, indeed," I babbled. "Shall we go?"

"By all means." He sounded not exactly annoyed but certainly unenthusiastic.

I felt a hot flush of embarrassment. Maybe he hadn't wanted to take me out tonight, and Gogi had talked him into it. I could just imagine the conversation.

"Cammy Chase? Who's she?"

"Somebody's got to take her," Gogi might have said—probably did, in fact—"and who else can I get?"

"If you'd rather—" I began impulsively, but he wasn't even looking at me.

"Good night, sir," he said wearily. "And Mrs. Duncan."

"Take care," said Mama, "and don't be late."

It was just what I didn't want her to say, especially in front of Eddie Arden. Probably she couldn't help it, being a mother and used to directing my footsteps. I didn't know why parents always talked about wanting their children to grow up independent and then insisted on veto powers in case they didn't approve of something. It wasn't honest, really, like letting a dog run free but only as far as the end of his leash. I gave Eddie an apologetic look, and he shrugged ever so faintly.

Mr. Duncan didn't seem to notice. He was gazing out into space with a little pucker between his eyes, I hoped not about me because I did not believe in stirring up tigers of any kind. It was bad enough that Mr. D. had to be here at all without his being annoyed with me besides. In any argument, I would be hopelessly outnumbered, with Mama on his side, as she surely would be. Probably, though, the frown was because of something at school, maybe who would teach the accelerated English classes or where he was going to get a new football coach in case this one got a bid from some junior college—the kind of things that he and Mama talked about all the time.

As Eddie and I headed for the front door, I could hear Mr. Duncan saying irritably, "I just don't see what else I can conscientiously do, Marian. When the chips are down, I have to stand with my teachers. If we—"

The door cut him off in the middle of a sentence that I was only mildly curious about. No affair of mine, naturally.

"Hi, Cammy."

It was Katy, being hauled along by Brandy, out for his evening canter. Her mouth fell slightly ajar when she saw Eddie.

"Oh, hi." I didn't even slow down. I couldn't stop and talk when I was going out on a date, could I, especially with

Eddie Arden? First thing tomorrow, I would run over and tell her all about it. "See you around."

Brandy, always cordial, lumbered up to me and threatened to put his paws around my neck.

"No!" Katy said sharply, and hauled mightily on his leash. I hastily climbed into Eddie's car as Katy and Brandy galumphed up the street. Eddie said, "What an ox!" which could refer to either Brandy or Katy—not that anybody who was entangled with Brandy could possibly look graceful. All the same, I gazed critically at Katy's departing figure. A few pounds off wouldn't hurt—a thought that I hastily quelled. I stole a look at Eddie's expressionless face as he whipped the car smoothly onto the new elevated expressway, dizzy with lights, like a swarm of fireflies flying in formation, and headed south toward the far side of town. At seventy miles an hour, only ten above the speed limit, we flew past Valencia's two new skyscrapers (twelve stories apiece), a huddle of dilapidated buildings waiting for urban renewal, a bakery tossing the yummy smell of fresh bread out into the night, and a few motels, elegant with lighted pools and rows of hovering balconies.

"Oh, it's all so fabulous!" I said, before I remembered that the people in Gogi's Gang probably didn't flip over the scenery, or if they did, they played it cool, cool, cool, keeping their rhapsodies to themselves.

I let the words drift away as Eddie slid down the exit ramp, along a dark street, and finally into a neon glare that spelled the Weary Why in a scrawl of light. It must be a sort of a nightclub then, perched on the outskirts of town, where there were still some blank spaces, with orange groves dim in the background and, alongside the parking lot, a real true pasture with a couple of horses grazing in it, shadowy silhouettes in the near darkness.

The door opened onto a blast of sound and color—electronic music pulsating from a brilliant stage, veering bands of light in psychedelic shades flickering over the rows of intent faces, a few childish yips, probably from the "screamies" too young to hang onto their cool, and, jammed together at a long table in the back corner, Gogi's Gang. I knew most of them by sight—Joellen and Mac, Sara and Randy, Dwight Campbell, who was Gogi's current boy friend, plus a couple of extra girls with no dates. I felt a quiver of excitement as Eddie steered me among the close-set tables.

"Hi!" I called, waving enthusiastically and immediately pretending I hadn't when I saw that everybody except Gogi, who was talking to Joellen, was staring at the stage as though hypnotized.

The chances were that nobody had heard me anyway above the thudding sound of the music. All the same, even rock players have to stop for breath once in a while. There was an abrupt hush, and Gogi's cool voice rang out.

"She'll definitely add something. Excitement. Danger. Oh, I have big plans for her."

Lucky her, whoever she was! The music roared again, and Gogi indicated by an arch of an eyebrow that she had seen us. I was especially glad that I had worn my new outfit, complete with green patent shoes with chunky heels and, for daytime, a pair of owl-eyed sunglasses with green frames.

"Welcome to the club," said Gogi, with a slantwise look at Joellen.

Gogi indicated a seat five places down from her. Her very best friends flanked her on either side, and I, the newcomer, was farther away—to be expected, of course. It was fantastic luck to be here at all, no matter where I came in the seating order.

> *"It isn't our world, no, no!*
> *It isn't our thing, yeh, yeh!"*

"Who's playing tonight?" I asked. After all, I ought to say something besides "Hi!"

"The Ironical I's," said Joellen, as though I should have known.

"Oh, of course." I pretended to drag the Ironical I's up from the depths of a memory positively jumping with rock musicians. They were belting out "Song of the Weary Why" with a good, strong beat.

"Not too great." Gogi pushed back her long hair, which immediately drooped back over her eyes again.

"Not as good as the William Tells," said Joellen.

"Or the Gold Standards," Sara echoed.

Gogi shrugged.

"The drummer's not bad."

I looked at him, striped in rapidly changing colors as the lights cut back and forth across the stage—a face that might have been faintly familiar if I had happened to know any drummers. He sounded great to me, and so did the rest of the Ironical I's. I looked around me, blank-faced, as though I had been here a hundred times. The Weary Why seemed to be a faint copy of the coffeehouses where the teeny-boppers hung out in New York—not that I had gone there either, but I had read a lot of newspapers while I was visiting my father and Dina. Still, the Weary Why was pretty sharp for Valencia, which wasn't all that metropolitan yet, even though it was growing like mad, part of the megalopolis that was supposed to be spreading all over Florida.

The Ironical I's chanted:

> *"It's all yours, Mother,*
> *Take it away, Father."*

27

Then came a final wailing cry:

"Why should we fight it? Why should we try?
This is the song of the weary why."

Thrilled to the core, I burst into loud applause, which earned me unreadable looks from Gogi and the rest. I hastily subdued my enthusiasm.

"They're rather good," I remarked languidly to Eddie.

"They'll pass."

Lighting a cigarette, he stared at the stage. Practically all the boys at school smoked, either out in the open or otherwise, but I was glad Eddie hadn't done it in front of Mr. Duncan, who might have felt it was his moral duty to advise against it, whether it ruined my social life or not. Gogi smoked, too, and so did lots of the other girls. So far I hadn't except once, back in junior high school when Katy and I had made ourselves sick on some of her father's cigarettes out back of the garage. Gogi held out her cigarette case.

"Be my guest," she said.

Surrounded by all those interested eyes, I hesitated. Why not, after all? I certainly wouldn't get lung cancer from just one cigarette, and Mama would never know the difference. I bent my head over Eddie's extended lighter. I coughed slightly, drew in a gulp of smoke, coughed again, and, feeling dizzy, hastily removed the cigarette from my mouth. Now if I could hold it more or less gracefully between my fingers and let it burn down without setting myself on fire, I would have established my independence—at least from Mama and Mr. Duncan.

"I saw a groovy dress in the window at Morrison's," Gogi murmured. "Honey-colored leather."

"Not on the rack yet?" asked Joellen.

The girls launched into a lukewarm discussion of clothes, to which I listened with an aloof expression. After all, I was wearing an Oakleigh Hill right that minute, a fact that I hoped Gogi remembered. The peculiar thing about my new dress was that Mama hadn't uttered a word about it except to say, "Very pretty," when I had expected her to come out with some remark about pouring money down a rathole, the way she had once when I had paid twice too much for a pair of shoes. Mr. Duncan hadn't said anything either, which just went to show how uninterested he was in what I did. It was rather disappointing, in a way, because I had been all ready to put up a big argument planned to bring through to them that it was nobody's business what I did with my own money. Probably something would be said sooner or later, but maybe not, because Mama and Mr. D. seemed terribly wrapped up in their own affairs just lately.

"Terrif . . . the Country Club . . . she's *the* original loser . . . the Last Resorts . . . definitely not a fab-type evening."

I listened, fascinated, as the talk, interspersed with long spells of silence except for the music, eddied around me. It was airy, inconsequential, faintly scornful, as though nothing was really very important. The music swerved to a finish, the Ironical I's vanished offstage for intermission, and people began stampeding out toward the lobby.

"Do we go outside?" Joellen turned to Gogi, who nodded.

"I guess."

I slid out from behind the table and gave a little gasp as the forgotten cigarette burned my finger. Under Gogi's amused look, I hastily snubbed it out in an ashtray. As we struggled outside, the horses, with their noses against the fence, stared curiously and then skittered back into the darkness as a car screeched out of the lot.

"Oh, they're frightened," I said. "Poor things!"

"Grim," said Eddie at my elbow. "Back in a second. I have to get some cigarettes out of the car."

I nodded, forlorn. Why couldn't I go with him?

"Should I wait here, then?"

He said, "Do that," and went, threading his way through the throng. I looked around for Gogi and the rest, but they had disappeared, too. I eased myself over beside a palm tree.

"Hi, Cammy."

It was Jay Vernon again, in the last place in the world I would have expected to find him. Still, talking to him would be better than waiting all alone until Eddie came back.

"What are you doing here?" I asked.

"Playing the drums. What's your excuse?"

"The drums? In the band?"

"No, in the pasture for the horses. You mean you never even noticed?"

"Well, almost." I remembered that fleeting moment of near recognition.

"Psychological study for my senior theme," said Jay.

"Already? When school hasn't even started?"

"I have to get the material where I can. Mental makeup of the rock generation. For instance, what brings you here?"

"Eddie Arden." A large chunk of ice crept into my voice. I didn't fancy being treated like a psychological case study.

"OK, OK. I was only asking."

He couldn't say I hadn't given him an accurate answer, but I didn't intend to go on about what a thrill it was to be here. Probably it was too much to expect, but I hoped I would get to come again because Eddie was much the most sensational boy I had ever gone out with. Everything that had happened, from my meeting with Gogi and Joellen at the Clothes Rack to this super place with its lights and music, was like a dream that I hoped I wouldn't have to wake up from right away. There was always the chance, too, that it might turn out to be not a dream at all. Gogi had said, "Welcome to the club"—a remark that had a permanent ring to it, if, of course, I could manage to look and act the way they would all think I should.

"Are your folks OK?" asked Jay.

"H'm?"

I didn't care about discussing the state of their health when I could be thinking about Eddie. I tried to blot out Jay's carroty hair, his bright blue eyes, and the thick sprinkling of freckles across his nose in favor of Eddie's cool assurance, but Jay was still there and still talking.

"Is your pop going to walk out with the rest of them?" he asked.

My pop? Naturally he meant Mr. Duncan, although "Pop" was about as far from my idea of him as I could imagine.

"Walk out? Out of where?"

He looked at me with elaborate patience.

"Look, kid, where've you been? In outer space?"

"In New York, actually, visiting my father."

Never mind adding that I hadn't heard a word from my father since I left, which was about par for the course. Maybe he thought the fifty dollars entitled him to a few months of silence.

"Nobody's told you about this stuff, with your pop— Mr. Duncan, I mean—in the business?" Jay gave me an unbelieving stare. "You gotta be kidding!"

I shrugged.

"So OK. I'm kidding."

Oh, why didn't Eddie come back and rescue me from all this? Jay kept on, though, relentless as an avalanche.

"The deal is, the teachers are planning to hand in their undated resignations, seeing they're not allowed to strike. That's what the mass meeting was about the other day. You remember that?"

I nodded like an obedient parrot—a distinctly bored one.

"So then they'll be all set to walk out if the state doesn't come through with some extra money for the schools. Mom's expecting to go, if she has to, and so's about everybody at Citrus. It's a way of putting on the pressure."

What was I supposed to do about it—burst into tears? A bell rang somewhere inside, and Jay began walking toward the entrance to the Weary Why.

"The call of the drum." He looked back at me. "The cash is another reason."

"Another reason?" I asked blankly.

"Why I'm here tonight." He put on a mirthless laugh-clown-laugh grin. "Worthy boy helping widowed mother. A sad story."

He flipped a nonchalant hand and walked off whistling what sounded like a hopped-up version of "I Got Plenty o' Nuttin'." Good riddance, too. What business was it of mine what the teachers did, even if one of them was Mr. Duncan? Alone in the milling crowd, I stared yearningly toward the parking lot, willing Eddie to come back right now, this minute. Usually I wasn't very self-conscious, but I did feel out of place standing here in the middle of a lot of strangers. Maybe I ought to go back to Gogi's table and just wait.

"Oh, Eddie!" I could hear the relief in my voice when he finally appeared beside me, but I hoped he couldn't hear it, too.

"Ready to go in?" he asked.

We finally caught up with the rest of Gogi's Gang in the crowded doorway.

"I don't know why *she's* so different," Sara was saying crossly. "Everybody else has to—"

"Cool it!" said Gogi. "I know what I'm doing."

Her voice sounded blurry, and her eyes were sleepy, but she was smiling faintly, like Mona Lisa, sort of, as we settled ourselves at our table again. The revolving bands of light shone on her blond hair and flickered across her still face.

> *"The weary why is our world, yeh, yeh!*
> (Thump, thump from Jay's drum)
> *The weary why is our thing—"*

"I simply adore this place!" I burst out impulsively—a child taking the first look at the tree on Christmas morning.

Gogi's Gang merely looked at me, silent and condescending. They must have thought I had never been anywhere in my whole life, to flip over a few lights and some not quite professional music. Still, they knew—or at least Gogi and Joellen did—that I had been to New York this summer, presumably among the teeny-boppers and hippies.

"Of course this isn't like the coffeehouses down in the Village," I might remind them, "but still—"

I decided against it. I would be silent and, hopefully, inscrutable, as though concealing in the depths of my being all sorts of enthralling experiences. As for their own air of boredom, surely they must like the Weary Why themselves or they wouldn't have come here in the first place.

"What do you think of the education crisis?" I demanded, throwing off childish things.

"What education crisis?" asked Sara, greatly uninterested.

"You didn't know?" I tried to parrot some of Jay's words, but somehow they didn't come. "Well, I suppose not. It's of rather specialized interest and quite complex."

So specialized that I wasn't interested myself and so complex that I couldn't go any farther on my own information. Conversation, except about clothes, seemed definitely not the thing here, anyway, rather to my relief. Gogi offered me another cigarette, which I declined, saying, "Have you ever tried Gauloises? But I don't suppose you can get them in Valencia."

All the better French spies smoked them, according to the paperback books I had read on the New York plane going and coming, but Gogi didn't look in the least impressed. The Ironical I's burst forth into a frenzied rendition of "Cut 'Em Off at Generation Gap," with the words bleated out by a bearded boy in a Nehru jacket.

"It must be terribly hot, especially in Florida," I observed above the tumult. "The beard, not the jacket, but maybe it's only glued on anyway."

That remark was greeted by an exchange of glances, accompanied by a tightening of the lips. Couldn't I remember about the inscrutable bit for even five minutes? I finished off my downfall by looking at my watch and springing up in a panic.

"Twelve o'clock! I have to go. If I'm not in by twelve-thirty, my mother'll—"

"Take her home, then, Eddie," Gogi ordered, and Sara muttered under her breath to Joellen "By all *means!* It's *twelve* o'clock."

"So nice of you to include me," I said with grim politeness to Gogi. "It was fun."

And so it had been—close to a miracle, even—until I had fouled things up by my unsophisticated chatter. As I stumbled miserably among the tables, with Eddie at my heels, the bearded boy onstage launched into "Never, No, Never, No, Never Again." Accurate, very. Tears stung my eyelids as I kissed the Weary Why good-by forever.

Three ✤✤✤✤✤✤

"Ter*ri*fic!" I said to my reflection in the mirror. "*Fab*ulous! Terrif! Fab!"

The effect wasn't right, though. The trick was to say "Terrif" and "Fab" as though maybe I meant it but probably I didn't—ironic, sort of. I tried it a few more times, but now the facial expression was all wrong. No expression at all was what I had to try for—a blank sheet of paper, an empty sky, a mirror with nobody looking in it.

"Terrif!" I repeated. "Fab!"

"Hi!" Katy bounced into my room. "What are you making faces at yourself for?"

"I wasn't," I said.

It was silly even to bother, since my chances of ever getting to try any of this out on Gogi's Gang added up to zero minus ten. Katy settled herself comfortably on the floor and held out a sack of potato chips, which I declined, remembering Eddie's remark about the ox.

"Eddie Arden!" said Katy. "How lucky can you get?"

Not half as lucky as she thought, but I wasn't going to go into that.

"Well, tell!" she demanded. "Where did you go, and who was there, and who said what?"

"The Weary Why," I said. "It's a night club, in a way."

"What was it like?"

"It was all right," I said in a voice as bored as Gogi's, now that it was too late. "Nothing special—music and a lot of psychedelic lights and a bunch of kids."

I just wished Katy would go on home and stop asking questions that were none of her business. Of course we always did talk over our dates in great detail, but I was in no mood for it this time. If I had been a sensational success, it would have been different, but I didn't want to be reminded that I had flubbed the only chance I would probably ever have with Gogi's Gang. I leaped up as I heard a faint sound above the hum of the air-conditioner.

"Was that the phone?" I rushed out into the hall but came back with my feet dragging. "No, I guess not."

"You think he might call?"

"Who knows?"

I knew, for one—or I was afraid I did. I didn't have the least reason to think I would ever hear Eddie Arden's voice again, except maybe as we passed in the hall or worked our way through the lunch line. Probably he wouldn't talk even then, since he seemed definitely not the gabby type. Maybe, of course, his silence last night had been because he had been too colossally bored to utter more than a few necessary words. I couldn't remember that any of Gogi's Gang had talked much, except for some very light chitchat about clothes and records and the music at the Weary Why.

"Who was there?" Katy asked. "Gogi's friends, I mean." I dutifully reeled off the list. "What were they like? Hippies, sort of?"

"Oh, no!"

Apparently they all bathed, and they were definitely well dressed. They didn't have the aura of genuine teeny-boppers, either, according to my New York reading on the subject, because they didn't hang adoringly around the musicians or get into a froth about psychedelic posters or try to shock people on the street with their noisy conversation. They couldn't even be labeled flower children—no flowers or beads (there was Jay's medallion, but that wasn't the same thing), nor perpetual talk about loving everybody. Unless they had developed a lot of ambition during the summer, they weren't even plain old high school kids trying to excel in everything so they could get into the good colleges that their parents wanted for them. So what were they, really? And what did it matter, anyway?

"They're just people," I finally said.

Katy gave up the inquisition and rummaged around in the bag for the last of the potato chips.

"I could help you paint that other wall before school starts," she said.

"Oh?" My room did look peculiar with three walls in pale blue and the fourth in a streaky mustard color that had once been gold. "Sometime. I'd have to try to match the paint."

I just couldn't get interested in finishing my room. After all, it had been like that for six months, and I didn't even notice any more. The hooked rug on the frame in the corner wasn't more than a quarter done either, but I had abandoned that even longer ago when I temporarily took up making seashell jewelry. Katy picked a scrap of potato chip off the floor and stood up.

"Mom says can you be ready to leave for the beach about 4:30 Friday," she said, blithely unaware of my irritable mood.

I hesitated. It was almost a tradition for me to go to the

Beckers' cottage on the last weekend before school began—a sort of farewell to summer.

"Well, thanks," I said, "but I can't make it this time."

"You can't?"

She waited for a long minute for me to say why I couldn't go, but I didn't. Let her think I had a couple more dates lined up with Eddie. Katy, the independent type, wouldn't be able to fathom anybody's missing a beach weekend to sit home waiting for a telephone to ring. I could hardly fathom it myself, but it was worth trying, since miracles, although uncommon, were not absolutely impossible. Katy finally seemed to realize that I wasn't going to explain.

"We'll miss you." She stood up, with a hurt look in her eyes. "I have to go home. Mom wants me to—" She didn't even finish the sentence, probably deciding that if I wasn't going to give a reason for what I did, she didn't have to either. "See you around."

"Want me to feed Brandy while you're gone?" I called after her—a completely phony offer made to ease my conscience, because I knew they always took Brandy with them to the beach, where he dug in the sand, collected antique fish, and galloped cheerily through the waves. Katy didn't even turn around.

"No, thanks," she said in a muffled voice. "He's going along, the same as usual."

I moped around home the whole long weekend, with never a sound from the telephone except a few calls for Mr. Duncan, who spent all day Saturday and most of Labor Day at school.

"Last-minute details," he told Mama—and me, too, I supposed, although my mind was definitely not on school, "so the first day won't be complete chaos."

When he wasn't at school, he was frowningly reading the

Valencia Press or prowling restlessly through the house.

"Aside from name-calling, the mass meeting doesn't seem to be getting much response from the state." He riffled through the *Press* for the umpteenth time. "Did you see the 'Letters to the Editor' column?"

"Now, Roger." Mama used her most soothing voice. "You can worry about all this later. Right now your job's to get Citrus High open and running."

"Good old Citrus High," I said—a remark that earned me a sharp glance from Mr. D. "Oh, I mean it. It's a great school."

The words were fine, but the intonation came out wrong—wrong from Mr. D.'s standpoint, anyway. I sounded, in fact, rather like Gogi, commenting on something that didn't interest her in the least. I hurriedly turned the conversation elsewhere.

"It's a wonder they didn't name it Pineapple Prep or Parson Brown Seminary."

Mr. D. laughed.

"Or Temple Tech," he said.

Somebody had had a terrific brainstorm when it was time to name things in our area, where in the beginning there hadn't been anything except orange groves. A lot of tourists probably thought the city was named for Valencia, Spain, but it wasn't. Valencia was a kind of orange, like Pineapple, Parson Brown, Temple, Mandarin, and Hamlin, all of which had streets named after them. Nobody had come up yet with a Grapefruit Avenue or a Lemon Boulevard, but there was an Orange Terrace out in one of the new subdivisions.

"Funny how things change," said Mr. D. "Valencia used to be strictly a citrus-oriented economy, but look at it now, with tourists and the military base and a lot of business and space industry."

Very interesting and instructive, but it didn't make the phone ring for me. Probably Eddie and the rest of Gogi's Gang were away for the weekend, even—horrible thought! —at the beach. I had probably made the mistake of a lifetime not to go with Katy. At least I might have caught a glimpse of the gang, but if they hadn't paid any attention to me, it would have been terribly humiliating, especially in front of Katy.

I saw her and her family, sunburned and windblown, coming home early Monday afternoon, but she didn't telephone to tell me all about her holiday. She didn't even walk Brandy past the house in the evening, probably on the theory that he had had enough exercise tearing up and down the beach.

"May I ride to school with you?" I asked Mr. D. on Tuesday morning.

He looked pleased, which he didn't need to. It wasn't his company I was craving; it was transportation.

"Sure. Glad to have you, if you don't mind leaving early."

"What about Katy?" Mama asked.

After all, we had been going to school together for eleven years, first on bicycles and then on the city bus, except that since Katy got her driver's license she took me in her mother's car whenever she could get it. I knew how to drive, too, but Mama seemed to need her car herself a good bit more than Mrs. Becker did.

"I think Katy has other plans," I mumbled.

"She could ride, too," said Mr. D., basking in his presumed popularity.

Probably going with Mr. D. wasn't the greatest idea in the world. Just because Mama had married the principal, I didn't want anybody to get the unrealistic idea that I was a teacher's kid. Most of them, I noticed, hung more or less on the fringes of high school society, suspected, probably, of being on the lookout for things to report back to their parents. Of course I had been just one of the common herd too, until the other night at the Weary Why, when I had risen to the heights for a little while before sinking to my own level again. I realized that I wasn't naturally the type for Gogi's Gang, but I felt sure I could have watched and imitated until I got the hang of the cool eye and the air of sophistication. I had even managed the voice perfectly naturally when I had been talking to Mr. D. about Citrus High.

Mr. D. and I didn't exchange more than a dozen words all the way to school. I was mourning for my lost opportunity at the Weary Why, and Mr. D. was probably worrying about whatever principals did worry about. In the teachers' parking lot, I said, "Thanks for the ride," and scuttled away before anybody could see me.

"Hey, hold it!"

Jay Vernon leaped out of his mother's car at the entrance to the parking lot. I didn't mind his seeing me with Mr. Duncan. After all, he was in the same situation, only more so—a real, true teacher's kid with no ifs and ands about it.

"I didn't see you at the Weary Why this weekend," he said, stepping unerringly on a very sore spot.

"I had other things to do," I said loftily. "Do you play there every night?"

"We have been. It'll be just a weekend once in a while from now on, I guess. There's not enough business during the week to justify live entertainment with the kids hitting the books again." He landed with a thud on another sore spot. "Where's Katy?"

I shrugged.

"She'll be along, I imagine."

Was it possible that Jay was getting interested in Katy? If so, she was welcome to him.

"I got a good idea for another poster to hang on Brandy if it turns out we need it."

"Oh?"

Maybe Brandy was the attraction, not Katy. Imagine being upstaged by a St. Bernard!

"I'm down this way," said Jay as we joined a milling crowd looking for homerooms. "Tell Katy I want to see her, huh?"

"If I see her myself."

I stiffened. Far down the hall I could see Gogi and Joellen. If I hurried, I could catch up with them, but if I did catch up, what would I say? Indecisive, I hesitated as though looking for a room number. Gogi and Joellen disappeared up the back stairs, and I rushed up the front way to my homeroom just in time to practically collide with them at the door.

"Oh, hi!" I said weakly. "Are you in here?"

"Not yet," said Gogi.

"We can't get through the door," added Joellen, deadpan.

"Oh, sorry."

I moved aside, a peasant making way for the gentry, and slid miserably into a seat in the farthest corner. I really wasn't going so great. Katy was mad at me, or so I supposed, and Gogi and Joellen had obviously checked me off as unworthy of their attention. I lifted my chin a little. I could manage without them, without any of them—big words to hide a big lump in my throat.

"Want to go shopping after school?" Gogi sat down unexpectedly in the back seat opposite mine.

"Huh? Are you talking to me?"

"Yes," she said levelly. "Want me to repeat the question?"

"Oh, no," I said. "I heard you the first time. I mean—" All this floundering around meant only that I couldn't believe my good luck. "OK. Where'll I meet you?"

"Parking lot, after school."

I nodded numbly and immediately started analyzing her motives. Maybe she was sorry for me, although she didn't seem quite the type to feel sorry for people or to do anything about it if she did. Maybe I hadn't been so awkward as I thought. I gave her a speculative look. It was hard to tell what was going on back of that smooth facade. The important thing was that I was getting another chance, which was more than I had expected. This time I must choose every word with care and use as few of them as possible.

Having to concentrate on how I acted kept the shopping trip from being much fun. As we went in and out of one store after another at Orange Plaza, I just couldn't keep my mind on lipsticks (would Pale Dream or Shining Moment go better with Gogi's hair) or pantdresses (the hot pink took Joellen's eye, but the orange might be a little newer) or yellow net stockings (just right with Gogi's new patent shoes). The surprising thing was that they didn't buy any of the things they admired. When Katy and I went shopping, we usually had something definite in mind and zeroed in on it without wandering off in all directions, but Gogi and Joellen were strictly lookers—or at least hard to suit.

"The Record Shop next," said Gogi.

That might not be a bad idea. I wanted to buy a record of "Song of the Weary Why" in case I never got back to the real Weary Why again, although I was feeling a little more hopeful, now that Gogi hadn't cut me off completely.

"Stereo or monaural?" the clerk asked.

"Monaural."

I hated to admit that we didn't have a stereo. My record player had cost only $17.95 and didn't even have a changer on it. Gogi and Joellen didn't seem to be paying any attention, though. They were idly flipping through the records in one of the far racks as I paid for mine.

"Anything special I can find for you?" the clerk asked.

"Do you have 'Black Is the Color of My True Love's Heart'?" asked Gogi, rummaging in her huge tote bag and coming up with a tattered list. "By the Silver Dollars?"

The clerk started leafing through the catalog.

"It's brand new," said Joellen. "You might not have it in yet."

"I guess not," said the clerk. "I don't find it listed. Sorry."

"We'll try later," said Gogi. "We're just looking, really. What did you get, Cammy?" She held out her hand for the sack with my new record. "Oh, the 'Weary Why.'" She called to the clerk. "Do you have this in stereo, too?"

"I'll have to check in the stock room."

"Look!" Gogi passed my record to Joellen, still flipping through the rack. "By the Double Martinis." She handed me back the sack with the record just as the clerk appeared with the stereo recording of "Song of the Weary Why." "Oh, well, I guess I won't take it after all, unless you have it by the Kangaroo Kings."

"But thank you, anyway," I chimed in, sorry for the clerk whom Gogi had kept chasing around after records that either hadn't been in stock or that Gogi hadn't bought after all the looking.

Probably the clerks were used to it, though, and of course stores were supposed to supply whatever service their customers needed. I looked anxiously at Gogi. I wouldn't want her to think that I had been criticizing her by thanking the clerk when Gogi hadn't. Luckily, her face held its usual non-committal look. Probably I was so afraid of disapproval that I saw it when it wasn't even there.

"I'll have to go home now," I said. "We have an early dinner." Anxious to please, I hastily added, "I can call my mother to get me if you're not through with your shopping."

"I'm ready," Gogi said promptly. "I didn't see anything really fab."

As I opened the door of Gogi's car, the sack with my precious record in it skidded out of my hands and began to slide to the pavement. I made a frantic grab for it.

"Oh, dear!" Records were supposed to be unbreakable, but nobody knew just how unbreakable. "Hey, there are two in here! The clerk must have made a mistake."

"Imagine!" Gogi held out a hand. "Let's see. Yours and 'Electronic Holiday.' I can use that if you don't want it."

Her lips had an ironic little twist as though she were secretly amused. I did wish I knew her well enough to tell when she was joking and when she wasn't—not that she seemed to be very strong for joking.

"I'll just run back and return it," I said. "Won't take a minute."

"Why bother?" Joellen asked. "The stores make enough on us, anyway."

"And next time she might make a mistake in her own favor and give you the wrong change," Gogi chimed in.

"But she didn't." Or I guessed she didn't. I looked from one to the other. "If you're in a hurry—"

"Oh, we'll wait," said Gogi with an air of sorely tried patience.

"I need to pick up a lipstick at the drugstore, anyway," said Joellen.

A lipstick! We had already looked at about a million lipsticks in three other places and not bought any.

"Meet you here in a couple of minutes, then," I said unhappily, aware of disapproval or at least impatience.

The girls probably thought I was terribly goody-goody even to dream of returning something that probably would never be missed, but I felt I had to do it. Mama had carefully explained to me when she married Mr. D. that I had to be very particular about how I acted, for fear of bringing criticism down on his head—just another example of how our entire lives were supposed to revolve around him now. I didn't know why I had to conform to somebody else's ideas of what was right and wrong instead of setting up my own standards. After all, everybody knew I wasn't really Mr. D.'s daughter, so why should it matter to him what I did?

When I came back from explaining to the clerk, who had seemed puzzled by the whole thing, Gogi and Joellen were waiting.

"Here!" Gogi tossed me a shining lipstick. "Present for your birthday, whenever it is."

"Wh-what? But—"

"Ran into a special," said Gogi, "and we thought it'd be clever if all the gang wore the same color lipstick."

"You bought them for everybody?"

"Like school colors," said Joellen. "Rah, rah."

Was it possible that in spite of everything I was really considered one of the gang? I took care to hide my sudden rush of pleasure.

"Well, thank you." I took the cap off the lipstick. "Do we start now?"

"Oh, absolutely." Gogi uncapped her lipstick, too. "One, two, three, go!"

The lipstick was Pale Dream, after all, so pale a dream that it was almost white, only faintly touched with pink. I preferred something brighter, but if Gogi liked it, it must be the latest thing. She had certainly spent enough time poring over it—and Shining Moment, too—four stores back. With mirrors in hand, we applied the new lipsticks—every movement identical, every expression intent and concerned. In spite of myself, I giggled.

"Like a ballet," I said—a remark that fell into silence as Gogi and Joellen concentrated on their art work.

"Lipsticks in Orange Shopping Plaza," I would call it, like "Murder on Tenth Avenue"—not that I knew the first thing about choreography. I was being a chameleon again, changing colors with every turn of thought. I had better keep concentrating on Gogi and how she acted if I wanted to stay in the swim. I was sure I hadn't improved my image in her eyes when I had insisted on returning the record. Still, Gogi and Joellen had bought me a lipstick along with the rest, so I still seemed to be more or less in the running. Probably, though, to Gogi half a dozen lipsticks were nothing; she had an air of having money to burn.

Mama was busy with dinner when I came in.

"Mama," I said, "what does Gogi Blakewood's father do?"

"Fix me some toasted almonds for the green beans, will you?" she asked. "Roger ought to be home any minute. Harold Blakewood? He has a big insurance agency, and he's active in a lot of civic things that have to have money raised for them. United Appeal, Fine Arts League, I don't know what all. Very well off, too. Why?"

"Just wondered. Gogi brought me home."

"Mmm." She took a look at my wan lips. "Where did you get the lipstick?"

"Gogi gave it to me. We went shopping, Gogi and Joellen and I. I bought a record."

"How was school?"

"All right." School was school, nothing that especially required comment.

"Katy stopped by. She brought back your beach coat that you loaned her." She hesitated. "You might call her."

"What about? She brought the coat back, didn't she?"

"No reason." Mama looked bewildered. "Did you and Katy have a fight about something?"

"Of course not," I said with what I hoped was sufficient fervor. "What would we fight about?"

"And by the way," Mama went on, carefully casual, "I want you to be as economical as possible for a while now."

I scowled. I might have known that the $39.95 dress wouldn't get by without comment. I leaped to my own defense.

"It was my money from Daddy. I guess I can spend that however I like."

"I wasn't talking about the money from your father," Mama said with chilly dignity. "I was referring to general spending—from Roger's salary."

So she was throwing it up to me that Mr. Duncan was paying most of my way! I marched into the dining room and set the silver down on the table in a clattering heap. I didn't know why Mama was so saving all of a sudden. Probably it was just one of her spells of economy when she got to worrying about how she—and Mr. Duncan, naturally—were going to manage my college bills next year, besides the leak in the roof and the creaking lawn mower that was going to conk out any time.

After supper, during which I spoke only when I was spoken to, I scraped the dishes in silence and went to my room to mope, playing "Song of the Weary Why" over and over until Mama stuck her head in the door and said irritably, "How about something else? Our nerves are bad enough already without—"

I didn't answer or even wonder why their nerves were shot just now. Wooden-faced, I turned off the record player. From the living room I could hear a man making a speech on television—something about education, just the kind of thing Mr. Duncan would think was the greatest. I closed my door with definite firmness, just missing slamming it. They couldn't stand my record player, but they didn't mind disturbing me with their tiresome TV programs. Oh, I was the third person in this house, all right!

I sat down at my dressing table and put on an extra-thick coat of Pale Dream lipstick. In the hall the telephone rang sharply, and I dived for the door. I crossed my fingers as I went. Would it be Gogi, already making plans for the Weary Why this weekend? Or maybe even Eddie Arden? With Gogi's Gang, anything seemed possible. I reached the telephone just one jump behind Mama.

"Sorry," she said. "Wrong number."

Four ✥✥✥✥✥

"Strictly stalling, that's all they're doing!"

"A study of educational needs! How many thousand studies do we have already?"

The buzz of teachers' voices rose above the smoke from our outdoor barbecue, where Mr. D., looking ridiculous in a chef's hat and a denim apron, was broiling hamburgers.

"I heard they have fifty thousand resignations all ready to be activated," the chorus continued.

How desperately boring! This was all education talk, more about the fight with the state, I supposed. I sighed, handed Mama another carton of hamburger buns, and wondered how soon I could retreat to my room, if at all. If there was anything that left me completely cold, it was this cookout, an annual event at which the principal and the faculty of Citrus High, with their families, got together for what they probably considered a real blast.

"But I don't have to be there, do I?" I had protested to Mama. "All those teachers!"

"Yes, you do have to be here! After all, you live right here. And don't speak that way about teachers, either. After all, your— Roger's one."

Mama had been acting terribly edgy lately, ready to argue about anything that she thought might be a slight for dear Roger. She also fussed a lot about my going to the Weary Why so much with Gogi's Gang. I couldn't imagine what she thought was going to happen to me there. All we did was sit and listen to the music and talk a little, not about anything important but just light remarks about kids in the audience or clothes or somebody's new car. It wasn't as though we were planning to riot or burn down any school buildings or anything like that. "We"—even though it had been only a month since Gogi first invited me to the Weary Why, I almost dared to think of myself as one of the gang. After all, it was always taken for granted that I would go with them, even when I didn't have a date. Almost always, though, Eddie picked me up—which just went to show that this was the age of miracles, after all. I still never felt sure of him because usually he didn't telephone until the last minute—which Mama thought was terribly rude.

"That's the way people do now," I explained in a kindly voice. After all, Mama hadn't been young for a long time and so could hardly be expected to be really with it. "Life isn't all that formal any more."

Sometimes, of course, Eddie didn't phone at all, and Joellen or Sara, in case they didn't have dates either, would stop by for me.

"Eddie had to go to a party his parents are giving," Gogi would sometimes report. "Veddy social."

Eddie's father was a major at the air base, so probably the party really was very social, not something as commonplace as a cookout for a lot of teachers. It was a comfort to know that I wasn't the only one who sometimes had to humor my —well, not my parents, actually. I didn't know just what one mother and one stepfather added up to, under the circumstances. I might have called them "my folks" if I had felt a little more cordial about the whole thing. At least I had friends of my own now, so it didn't matter quite so much how things were at home—or did it? Still, I couldn't help feeling left out when Mama and Mr. Duncan would sit in the living room talking and laughing—not so much of the latter just lately, though—while I played records in my room.

"Want to go to the movies?" Mr. Duncan would ask me every so often or, "Let's run over to the driving range," or, "The Brookses want us all to come over and try their new pool."

Psychologically it was very sound—the stepparent establishing empathy with the child and all that—but I always made up an excuse about doing my homework or expecting a telephone call or having to wash my hair. I felt as though I were just another duty for Mr. D.—one of Mama's unavoidable encumbrances. Besides, Gogi and her friends didn't go running around with their families all the time. The generation gap was a whole lot too wide to jump, even if there had been anything especially fascinating on the other side.

"Where shall I put this, Marian?" Mrs. Hopkins, who was an old friend of Mama's and taught math, came rushing up with a big bowl of potato salad. "Oh, hello, Cammy. What's the current project?"

"Project?"

"Remember when you refinished your desk for home ec credit? And made the bedspread? And painted all that pottery?" Mrs. Hopkins burbled. "I've always loved to come over here just to see what you were doing." She turned to Mama. "So many young people nowadays just don't have any constructive interests."

I had news for her. I didn't have any constructive interests any more either—not the kind she had in mind, anyway. What was the matter with just living along, the way Gogi's Gang did, and leaving the constructive bit to the older people who thought it was so great?

"Well, I don't have anything special going right now," I mumbled. "With school and all—"

That touch about school ought to go over big with a teacher, although the truth was that I hadn't really been hitting the books much lately, what with the Weary Why and going shopping so much with Gogi and Joellen. I wasn't worrying, though. I could stoke all the information in before the six weeks' tests and get through all right.

"School's a drag. Let's face it," Gogi was always saying. "But it calms the parents."

Gogi made a big thing out of her folks' letting her do what she liked and go where she pleased—no telephoning to say she'd be late, no asking whether she could go wherever it was.

"Oh, I'm the lucky one!" she said in her noncommittal voice. "All this civic stuff keeps them out of my hair."

From the number of times their names appeared in the paper, the Blakewoods must be members of every organization in town, real big shots if that was the way to measure bigness, which maybe it was and maybe it wasn't. Joellen had things pretty much the way she wanted them, too, but for a different reason. Her mother, who was divorced, ran home parties for a cosmetic firm, so she was away most evenings.

"Does she rack up!" Joellen had once said. "And money's what you have to have."

Her mother must have really been raking it in because Joellen always had the latest in clothes, like Gogi, and lots of them. As for me, Mama was still clamping down on my spending, so I was having to do some sewing again to keep up with the crowd.

"You have plenty of clothes, anyway," Mama insisted. "You can't wear more than one dress a day."

"Monday, Tuesday, Wednesday, Thursday, Friday, Saturday, Sunday. Then repeat from the beginning. People will know what day it is from what I have on."

"Sad." Mama was distinctly unsympathetic nowadays. "Mix and match them then—Thursday's skirt with Monday's blouse. That'll fool this fashion board you go around with."

I never bothered to answer her little digs at Gogi and the rest because if I got into a real true argument, she might forbid me to go out with them at all, and I wasn't sure I would have the courage to defy her, much less Mr. D., who would probably get into the act, too, although he had never yet uttered a word of criticism to me. Gogi and Joellen really had it made. With mothers who didn't try to run their lives, they never had to argue or defy, although I didn't doubt they would do it if they ever needed to. I couldn't imagine their mothers saying, "No, you can't go," the way I was sure Mama would if she got excited enough. I just had to remember that the soft word was my best weapon.

"Oh, I'm doing a little sewing," I told Mrs. Hopkins. Why spoil her evening by denying all the activities she seemed to get such a charge out of? "Remnants."

Remnants were all I could afford out of my current allowance, which was plenty skimpy now under Mama's economy regime. My sewing was turning out all right, though, and I always stitched in a label from an old dress when I got through, so Gogi, in case she looked, would never know that practically all my clothes were homemade, except, of course for the famous Oakleigh Hill. The sewing was another reason why I was behind in school—a fact that I was keeping from Mama and Mr. Duncan. After all, as long as I learned the stuff sometime, there was no need to stick to a strict schedule.

"Come and get 'em while they're hot!" Mr. Duncan called. "Hamburgers right here, salad, dessert, and coffee on the long table."

It certainly wasn't a very *chic* cookout—nothing like the steaks and avocado salad that Gogi had once casually mentioned on the menu of her parents' parties. Besides, the Blakewoods had a swimming pool, which I had seen when I had stopped by once with Gogi to pick up something. I had never been in it yet, but Gogi had invited us all to a swimming party for Sunday afternoon.

"We have to do something, don't we?" she had said. "And the Weary Why's not open."

I had already gone with her to shop for a new bikini. After trying on at least a dozen, she had apparently settled on a darling pink polka dot at Albin's, but at the last minute she had decided against it.

"I want to look around some more," she had told the salesgirl from the welter of suits around her. "Here, you might as well put most of them back on the rack. You help her, Cammy."

I didn't know how she ever accumulated the wardrobe she did, with all the time it took her to make up her mind, but whatever she appeared in was absolutely perfect for her, so maybe it paid to shop around.

"Hand me some more buns," Mama murmured as the teachers lined up to fill their plates. "I wonder where Marie Vernon is. She was supposed to bring another chocolate cake." I thought it was terribly inhospitable for Mr. D. and

Mama not to provide all the food themselves, but nobody ever asked for my opinion any more. "Oh, there she is!"

Mrs. Vernon hurried around the corner of the house.

"Sorry to be late, but Jay was held up at work."

Work? He must have a job somewhere besides at the Weary Why, where there wouldn't be any music in the afternoon. He set the cake down on the table and gave me a wide grin.

"Snappy, huh? Boy, do you pick 'em!"

"H'm?" I lifted a questioning eyebrow.

"The shirt, girl!" He threw out his chest and flexed his arms. "Am I the man of distinction!"

He was wearing the gaudy red-and-yellow plaid shirt that I had angrily picked out for him at Albin's the day my entire life had been changed by my running into Gogi and Joellen at the Clothes Rack. The shirt looked just as horrible as I had hoped it would. The red fought with Jay's carroty hair, and the yellow fought with the red—altogether a very successful purchase from my point of view.

"Cool," I said, "real cool."

"Yeah." From his tone of voice I almost thought he knew exactly what I had had in mind when I bought the shirt. "You're campaigning for Katy, I guess?"

So now what? I didn't even know Katy was running for anything. Jay, all eagle-eyed, seemed to read my confusion in my face.

"For vice-president of Student Council," he said. "The girl that had the job moved away."

"Oh. Well, goodie for Katy!"

I felt faintly guilty whenever I thought about Katy, which wasn't very often any more. With Gogi and the rest taking up practically all my time, I hardly ever even saw

Katy. She had come over a couple of times, but once I had been in the shower and once I had had to leave in five minutes because Joellen was picking me up.

"Sorry about that," I had said. "See you soon, though."

"Oh, sure."

Her voice told me that she doubted it, and she had never come back. I really had meant to go and see her, but I hadn't managed to get there, even only a block away. The truth was, I hadn't tried very hard.

"How about making a speech for her in assembly?" Jay asked. "I'm lining up some talks for next Wednesday. I may even get Brandy to parade for her during lunch hour."

He was certainly a great one for campaigns and crusades. In a minute he would be sounding off about the teachers' troubles, too, no doubt.

"Oh, I couldn't," I said. "I—I'm not so crazy about making speeches."

I could imagine how Gogi would react if she saw me standing up on the platform carrying a banner and yakking away about *Katy Becker for Vice-President*.

"I don't get it," Jay blurted. "I thought Katy was your best friend."

"Oh, I have a lot of friends," I said airily.

What was so surprising was that now I really did have— at least a dozen, which should make up for having lost a father and a mother and a sense of belonging somewhere.

"Lucky you!" Jay's voice was sharp. "Lots of friends, and most of them brand new."

"And so?"

What business was it of his, anyway? He was just jealous because he didn't have any exciting friends himself. I remembered, almost too late, that he was my guest—not mine, really, but at least a guest at the house where I ate and slept.

"Here, have a hamburger and some salad and stuff," I said.

When our plates were loaded, I hurried him around the corner of the house to the concrete bench beside the fish pool, away from all the chatter. If we were going to argue about my friends, I wanted to be out of range of all those teachers. I didn't even wait for any more remarks from him but began talking myself.

"I have fun," I said, "more fun than I ever had—and why not? Let the grownups manage things. It's their world."

"That's what I hear, every week at the Weary Why.

> " 'It isn't our world, yeh, yeh,
> It isn't our thing, no, no!'

"It's the only world we've got to work on, for Pete's sake!"

"Eat," I said, "and build up your strength." I paused. "What could we accomplish, anyway—just a bunch of kids? Nobody'd pay any attention to us."

"It's good practice. Who do you think is going to run things ten years from now?"

"Oh, ten years! Time enough to think about that later. We're only young once."

"Yes, and some of us are going to be young all our lives if we don't watch it."

I didn't see much point in talking about accomplishing things, anyway, when I didn't know of anything I wanted to accomplish except to stay friends with Gogi's Gang and to keep on going to the Weary Why. If Jay wanted to redesign the world, let him go ahead.

"I'll get us some more hamburgers." Jay swallowed the

last bite of his. "And some of Mom's cake—best devil's food around."

"OK." I headed his mind in another direction and hoped it would stay there for a while. "What kind of job do you have now? Your mother said—"

"I'm helping a guy paint the trim on his house—just a few days' work."

"What! Nothing about the psychology of the rock generation?"

"I've got plenty of material for that, believe me!" he said. "Term paper's half written already."

"And not due until after Christmas! You're really organized."

"I have to do stuff when I can, between whatever jobs turn up."

Sometimes on the weekends he and the Ironical I's still played at the Weary Why, although new groups were always coming and going—the Major Disasters, the Groovy Greats, the Last Chances. I was getting fairly expert at tossing off bright little comments about them— "Very psychedelic!" or "Schmaltzy, ugh!" or "Engulfment, and I *mean!*"

Jay got up and reached for my plate.

"What all do you want?"

"Just a hamburger and the cake, please."

Maybe he would get sidetracked talking to somebody else and wouldn't come back to prod my conscience with his critical remarks. I didn't feel guilty about anything except Katy, but apparently she was doing all right without me if she was running for office with any hope of winning. It was just too ridiculous to imagine I would give up Gogi and the gang in favor of walking Brandy and hooking rugs and electioneering and getting into this teachers' fight, as Jay probably thought I should. With Gogi's Gang, I felt part of something; at home I didn't, or even with Katy, who was, after all, only one person instead of a whole crowd. Inside, the telephone rang, and I scooted through the patio door to get it.

"Cammy?" My heart gave a big leap. "Eddie. Pick you up in half an hour?"

"Well, I—"

Mama had certainly said I had to attend this cookout, but, on the other hand, she hadn't actually said I had to stay all evening. Maybe in this crowd I wouldn't be missed until I was safely away, and I could leave Mama a note to say I was going.

"All right. Wait for me around the corner on Mandarin, please. We have a million cars parked in front."

"Will do. Parents giving you trouble?"

"Oh, no. Not at all," I said hastily. "See you."

I looked at myself critically in the hall mirror. I wished I could change into a livelier outfit, but of course I couldn't or Mama would want to know why. I hastily scribbled a note— "Gone with Eddie. Back by twelve!"—and tucked it into my pocket, to be propped up on top of the dishwasher at the last minute. I knew Mama wouldn't like it, but I wouldn't like staying home either.

In a way, it would be a relief if Eddie didn't pick me up at the house, for once. He always sounded perfectly polite, but I couldn't help feeling nervous for fear Mr. Duncan, who was smart in an academic way or he wouldn't be the principal of Citrus, might catch on one of these times that Eddie's innocent-sounding "Yes, sirs" and "No, sirs" were really a satire on the manners admired by adults. Then if Mr. D. said anything about it, such as not liking Eddie's attitude, I would be ruined as far as future dates were concerned. Still, he could hardly complain about all those "sirs"—or maybe he could. Mr. D. had once warbled in an unrestrained bass at breakfast:

> *"It isn't the words,*
> *It's the music,*
> *It isn't the bread,*
> *It's the baloney."*

How absolutely dopey could a person get?

Strictly for propaganda purposes, I trotted outside again to see if Mama needed any help. Jay, balancing two wedges of cake and some hamburgers on a pair of paper plates, intercepted me.

"We'll have to eat up," he said, "so's not to miss the TV broadcast. Big announcement from the state on the education thing."

"OK." With everybody parked in our living room listening to the word, it would be a lot easier to leave without anybody's noticing, even Mama. "I have to go pretty soon, anyway."

"So do I, after. I promised to help Katy with some campaign posters while Mom's working on the cleanup detail. Sure you don't want to come and help us?"

I shook my head.

"I have a date." I didn't know why I bothered to add anything beyond the plain fact, but I did, as though I were justifying myself, which I certainly didn't have to do. "After all, it's the weekend."

"Sure." He didn't even seem interested. "Look, don't think I'm saying this to get Mom in good with the boss, but Mr. Duncan's quite a guy." So all right! Everybody to his taste. "He's got the kids at school right with him."

"Really?"

I didn't know why Mr. D. was such a success at school—

if he really was—when he couldn't make any impression on me at home. Of course I didn't give him much of a chance. I was off and away every minute I could be now that I had a life of my own and didn't have to depend on a couple of people who probably preferred to be by themselves, anyway. Jay looked at his watch.

"Five to eight. Everybody's going in."

I wouldn't even have gone inside to listen except that I wanted Mama to see me around for as along as possible. I hurried to my room to pick up my tote bag, stuck it out of sight behind Mama's big jar of peacock feathers in the hall, and stood with Jay in the doorway to the living room.

"Do you and Jay want to bring in some of the folding chairs from the patio?" Mama asked.

"Yes, ma'am," I said, pleased that she had noticed I was there. "Right away."

"Buy Parsons' peanuts by the jar," the TV was proclaiming, "Crisper, fresher, best by far!"

"H'm," Jay said. "Maybe we could think up a jingle for Katy's campaign—a strolling quartet. Can you sing?"

"No," I said firmly.

"I'll get some of the glee club kids, then." He grinned. " 'All the way from here to Haiti/ There's no one greater than our Katy.' How does that grab you?"

"Ugh!"

" 'Ugh' the verse or 'ugh' the sentiment?"

"Oh, the verse, naturally."

"Poets always have it rough. In other words, 'The verse/ Couldn't be worse.' "

"The chairs," I reminded him.

Even with the extra chairs and our living room and adjoining family room as big as they were, lots of people still had to sit on the floor or lean against the walls.

63

"Shhh!" Everybody fell silent as the governor appeared on the screen.

"I forgot my lipstick," I whispered to Jay. "Back in a minute."

Intent on the TV, he nodded. I didn't rush back right away but I did wait for nearly fifteen minutes more until I heard the voice of Parsons' Peanuts again, followed by the rise and fall of teachers' voices. Then I hurried down the hall, retrieved my tote bag, and headed for the door.

"Hey," said Jay, "you missed it. He's calling a special session of the legislature in January to deal with the educational crisis."

"This is good?"

He shrugged.

"Who knows? No walkout for a while, anyway. Presents for Christmas, etc., etc."

Wonderful! Marvelous! Maybe now Mama would stop pinching the pennies quite so hard—if the prospect of no paycheck for Mr. D. had really been the cause of all her economy. I hadn't bothered to find out. I hadn't even wondered whether Mr. D. was planning to walk out with his teachers if they actually did walk out. What did it matter to me what he did?

"I have to leave." I had a sudden inspiration. "Are you going down to Katy's now?" He nodded. "May I walk along with you? Eddie'll be waiting for me around the corner."

"Oh, sure."

He gave me a curious look, which I answered with a flurry of explanations.

"There're too many cars out front, and he wouldn't want to double park and— He said he'd pick me up here, but I said to—"

"Naturally." Jay's voice was dry. "I understand."

Probably he did, which made me regret my explanations even more. I caught Mama's eye and gestured toward Jay and then toward Katy's house. Mama nodded enthusiastically, as I had known she would, and I walked triumphantly out. We were nearly to Katy's before I remembered that I hadn't left the note to tell Mama where I was really going.

"Jay," I said, "would you mind— I forgot to leave word with Mama about where I'd be and—"

"And you want me to do the dirty work for you," he said evenly.

"All right!" I flared. "Don't, then!" I dug into my tote bag and dragged out the note. "All I'm asking is for you to give her this when you go back to pick up your mother. What's so terrible about that?"

He held out his hand resignedly.

"OK. Consider it done."

"And thank you," I said, "so, so much."

That last bit of sarcasm was probably unnecessary, but Jay hadn't been exactly cooperative or even agreeable. I rounded the corner at a gallop, fluttering my fingers at Jay as he headed across under the street light for Katy's. I was already late, what with trying to get away and arguing with Jay about the note. Eddie would be absolutely furious, if he had even waited. He was there, though, parked without lights under a big water oak. The door on my side swung open the instant I got there, I scrambled in, and the car jerked into abrupt motion, barely missing Brandy, who was crossing the street toward home.

"Where've you been?" Eddie demanded. "You said half an hour, right?"

Five ✣✣✣✣✣

"Sorry about that," I said as Eddie took the corner with his usual shriek of tires. "The house was full of teachers, and I had to sort of ooze out."

Gogi or Joellen would just have shrugged, without uttering a word of explanation, but I always felt I must keep Eddie soothed for fear he might not come back. Considering that he had called me at the very last minute, I didn't think he was in any position to criticize me for being a little bit late. I didn't know what the rush was, anyway. The Weary Why would be there all night, which was longer than I would be able to stay.

From the way Eddie jerked the car around the corners and slammed on the brakes at the stop streets, I knew that something more than just my being late was bugging him.

"Some days you can't win," I said, receiving only silence in reply.

He was taking a terribly roundabout way to the Weary Why—in fact, approximately around the world—but I didn't say anything about that either. He kept weaving among a snarl of short streets—left, right, right,—until I had no idea where we were.

"This Jay Vernon," Eddie finally muttered. "Where'd you pick him up?"

My spirits zoomed like a balloon rising into the clouds. Even Jay had his uses if Eddie was actually jealous of him and blamed him for making me late for our date. I hesitated. Would it be better to reassure Eddie or to let him wonder, as Gogi would probably have done? I decided on a little of each.

"Oh, he came to the cookout with his mother and walked down to the corner with me."

Nothing about Jay's being on his way to see Katy, nothing about her campaign for Student Council, nothing about my using Jay as a way of getting out of the house.

"Oh?"

His voice was completely noncommittal, and his expression, as usual, didn't tell me anything. If only he would gnash his teeth or yell to give me some idea of what he was really thinking! Even his small burst of annoyance at my being late was very unusual—not, I thought, because he was never irritated but because the aloof air that I was slowly achieving, too, was the trademark of Gogi's Gang, setting them apart from all the burblers and chatterers like Katy, and, yes, me, too, before I became one of the gang myself. Sometimes, though, I wished for a little more animation—a traitorous thought that I hastily pushed to the back of my mind. What was the matter with me? A few weeks ago I would have thought my present position was just south of seventh heaven, and now here I was picking away at something that didn't really matter.

"Hey, give a look!" Eddie's voice held a tinge of interest.

I couldn't see anything unusual about this quiet street with its row of covered trash cans waiting for the weekly pickup, but Eddie had ideas of his own.

Swooping to the left side of the street, he reached out of his open car window, lifted the cover off a trash can, and shied it down the old brick pavement with a tremendous clatter. Clang! Clang! Clang! Three more lids followed the first before porch lights began to go on all down the block. Eddie ran an obstacle course among the lids that now littered the street and turned the next corner in search of more trash cans. He missed on the first one and overturned the whole can, with a crash of bottles and a clank of galvanized metal.

"Garbage-can polo!" he muttered as he sent a few more lids flying.

His eyes were intent, and a tight little smile curved his lips. More porch lights went on, a couple of people stepped to their doors, and somewhere a police siren started up, wailing nearer and nearer.

"End of chukker, end of game," said Eddie.

The tires howled as he made the next corner at high speed, turned left again, whizzed through the light just as it was turning red, and whirled along more strange streets before turning off on a narrow lane and stopping in deep shade. Far away, the sirens faded and died.

"How about that!" His lips quirked. "That woke up the natives!"

"Wow!"

I leaned back limply, feeling as though I had witnessed a totally unexpected eruption of Vesuvius. This wild attack on the trash cans was the last thing I would have expected from the undemonstrative Eddie.

"The age of rebellion," Mr. Duncan had once said about a brief sit-in at the start of school. I hadn't paid any particular attention to it—probably something about the long-hair rules or not being allowed to eat off-campus at noon. "It's a phase the young go through, like measles, but some recover fast and others get complications."

That was what was so tiresome about adults—the constant inspection, as though we were bugs under a microscope, the endless analysis, the patient "Oh you'll get over it" attitude or the not so patient scoldings. Still, it would be interesting to know what was bothering Eddie. Jay, with his research on the psychology of the rock generation, might know, but naturally I wouldn't dream of asking him. Who cared, anyway?

"Hey!" Eddie hauled a flashlight out of the cluttered glove compartment. "Do you have any of that eyelash goop with you?"

"Mascara?" I rummaged in my tote bag. "Yes, I do have."

I didn't actually need mascara, with my naturally dark lashes, but Joellen had showed up one day with some for everybody, unusually generous samples with the Albin label on them, and so I carried mine around for luck. When I was with the others, I sometimes dabbed away at my lashes—a sort of tribal gesture to show that I belonged with Gogi's Gang.

"Let's have it." He motioned me out of the car and got out himself. After glancing in all directions along the dark street, he whipped around to the back of the car. "OK. Hold the flashlight on the license plate." He took the little spiral brush out of the mascara tube and looked at it helplessly. "You do it, and I'll hold the light."

"What? Do what?"

He pointed a finger at the numbers on the plate.

"See if you can make the sevens look like ones. I don't think anybody saw the license, but just in case—"

I dabbed obediently at the gray numerals, blending the

tops of two sevens into the dark background. The sirens were wailing somewhere again, but surely this must be a different deal. A few garbage can lids would hardly cause all that commotion.

"Too bad the plates aren't red this year," I said. "Lipstick's easier to put on."

"Yeah." Eddie stepped back to look. "That's great, real great."

"The Mascara Monet," I said.

He snapped off the flashlight.

"Can you drive?"

"Sure. Can't everybody?"

"Good. I'll scrooch down in the back, just until you get us a little farther away."

"Well, I don't know. I—"

"Ah-h-h, nobody's going to bother a girl. Are you chicken or something?"

I drove, uneasy in a strange car.

"Take a right here," Eddie said from the vicinity of my right ear, and "Left at the corner," and "Straight ahead to the end." I was thoroughly confused by another maze of small streets, but at least I was thankful not to be in a lot of traffic as I clutched the wheel with damp hands and felt for the brake at every stop sign. I was afraid to go very fast, and Eddie muttered something under his breath. Finally he said, "Left, now, and turn off the lights. I'll take it."

"Do that," I said crossly, stopping the car and sliding to my own side.

He climbed over from the back seat and took the wheel. Immediately he was the Eddie I was used to, lazily self-assured, carelessly amiable. He pulled me closer to him on the seat.

"In the clear!" he exulted. "I wouldn't bother, only the

old man said one more ticket and I'm grounded for a month. Where'd I be without wheels, I ask you?"

Sitting at home, and so would I except when Gogi or Joellen picked me up. Naturally, though, it was Eddie's company that I wanted, his profile against the light, his arm around my shoulders when he wasn't using it to drive with.

"Ran a red light coming after you," he went on, "and there was a cop just down the block, so I had to take off fast. How unlucky can you get?"

"Very." Between the red light and the trash cans, we had had an extended tour of half the back streets in Valencia.

"No problem now, though. We've got it made."

If he was already on probation at home, I didn't think the trash can caper was exactly clever, but probably he had had a big fight with his father before he came tonight and had to get his anger worked off some way. What did a few trash can lids matter, anyway? At Halloween people did lots worse things, and nobody thought anything about it.

"Who's playing at the Weary Why tonight?"

I reminded him in a roundabout way that Gogi was expecting us there.

"Whoever it is, they won't be real great." The note of discontent was back again. "I heard the Silver Spur out on Kumquat Drive really has it—way-out stuff."

"Then why don't we—"

"They won't let us in."

"Too young?"

"Yeah. They're scared we might try to order a drink."

Plenty of people at the Weary Why, including some of the boys in Gogi's Gang, kept bottles out in their cars. Maybe Eddie did, too, but he had never offered me a drink. I hoped he wouldn't because I wasn't sure whether I would take it or not, and I didn't want to have to decide. One of the troubles about trying to be grown up was having to make up my mind about things when I wasn't really ready.

Katy and I always used to talk about stuff like that—cigarettes and drinks and whether to kiss our dates good night—but of course I was completely out of touch with Katy now. I was the one who had graduated to Gogi's Gang and the Weary Why, while Katy had stayed behind in the same old world.

For just a minute I felt a wave of homesickness for Katy and Mama and the way things used to be before Mr. Duncan threw everything off balance by marrying Mama. Without Gogi's Gang to fill the time, I didn't know how I would have made it. *And what about Katy?* something deep down inside me asked—probably the conscience that people were always supposed to be holding mental dialogues with. *How did Katy feel, now that I didn't go to the beach with her any more or help her walk Brandy or talk over everything that happened to us?* I pushed the thought away. I was beyond all that now, moving confidently among the "in" people—or at least medium confidently. The trick was not to talk too much or with too much enthusiasm. I could always tell when I had been too eager by the little quirk of amusement on Gogi's face and the glances that darted back and forth among the rest of the gang.

"You have to be careful not to bubble," I would have told Katy in the old days when I was still telling her things. "You have to practice a sophisticated expression, too, as though you'd been around a long time and weren't surprised by anything much."

"Deah, deah! Not even by gold-plated water faucets and forty-dollar dresses?"

I could almost hear her saying the words. Katy always got the message without a lot of explanation—and why shouldn't she, with all the practice she had had? We had been talking to each other for a good fifteen years and yammering away in our playpens even before that.

We pulled into the parking lot at the Weary Why, and I tried to push Katy out of my mind. People didn't usually stay best friends forever, anyway. They practically always went off in different directions sooner or later—one of the facts of life—and the Weary Why and Gogi's Gang happened to be in my direction. If Katy wanted to get involved with this silly Student Council election and Jay Vernon wanted to take up every crusade that came along, like the teachers' thing, it was their own affair, except— I didn't know except what, really, but I wished it would go away, that little sliver of doubt that kept scratching at my mind like a sandspur sticker just under the skin.

"The Angry Apes." Eddie gestured toward the sign in the lobby of the Weary Why. "New outfit."

"Great," I said. It was a useful word with many shades of meaning, depending on the tone of voice.

The Angry Apes, perched on long-legged stools of various heights, were letting themselves go with a burst of electronic music that boomed through the room and bounced off the ceiling.

A voice wailed:

> *"Angry with rich men, angry with poor men,*
> *Angry with beggarmen, angry with thieves,*
> *Angry with doctors and lawyers and chiefs,*
> *Mad at the world, and I'll never forgive*
> *Nor ever forget for as long as I live."*

Gogi, tapping her long silvery nails on the table as Eddie and I settled ourselves among the twisting ribbons of light, looked mad at the world, too.

"Swimming party's off." Her voice was tight with anger. "I *told* them I wanted the pool tomorrow, and they said OK, so now they've invited a bunch of people themselves." Her lip curled. "How often do I ever ask to have *my* friends? And when I do ask— Forgot, they said."

Her eyes glittered behind the new set of false eyelashes she had appeared with a few days before.

"Genuine ranch mink," she said, which I didn't doubt they were.

"We'll come some other time, then," I said soothingly.

She glared at me.

"Some other time! Do you think I'd ever even dream of asking again? They can keep their old pool, and—"

This was anti-parent day, for sure—first Eddie and now Gogi, although I thought Eddie's fit of temper went a little deeper than a mere fight with his father about traffic tickets, and maybe Gogi's did, too.

"We'll have our party in spite of them." Gogi's smile was triumphant. "I know a marvelous place to swim."

"Terrif!" said Joellen.

"When?" asked Sara.

"Why not right now?" Gogi dropped her cigarettes and her new enamel lighter into her tote bag, ready to go.

"I don't have a suit with me," I said.

Gogi shrugged.

"So what? Eddie can take you home to get one."

"After all the trouble I had getting out in the first place?"

Gogi gave me a pitying look—poor little ol' Cammy, with her parents always on her back!

"We'll stop by my house then. You can borrow one of my bikinis." She looked questioningly at Sara and Joellen. "You, too, if you want. I've got loads."

It must be great to have so many suits that you could scatter them like confetti among your friends. I had only one, and it wasn't the last word either.

Eddie went into a huddle with Dwight and Mac and Randy. Mac had a pair of swimming trunks in the back of his car, and so did Randy, but Eddie said, "I'll stop and pick up a pair at the Discount Center—save driving all the way out to the base."

"We've got all night," said Mac.

Maybe they did, but I didn't. In fact, I had only about three hours before I had to be home—before I had said in my note that I would be home, that is.

Eddie got up as the Angry Apes launched into "The Gold Medallion."

"I got it for bravery, my gold medallion.
I stood in the front row where the night sticks hit me.
As they dragged me away to the paddy wagon
My darling slipped me the gold medallion.
'For bravery,' she whispered,
'This gold medallion.' "

"Meet you all at Gogi's in a while, then?" asked Eddie. "Come on, Cammy."

"What a dopey song!" Gogi slid out of her seat, heading for the door.

The words might be dopey—all about some more people out to buck the world—but the beat did get to a person as the drums thumped like night sticks whacking on somebody's skull and the guitars crescendoed into the wail of police sirens. Jay would probably be mad about it, both words and music.

From the parking lot I could see the two horses standing in the pasture, silhouetted against the sky. A little way down the sandy lane marked Dead End, the lights from the Weary Why picked out a few oranges that were just starting to show a trace of color against the dark leaves. Farther still, beyond the shadowy mass of trees, there might be more orange groves, maybe a house, maybe a lake. As Eddie and I followed the other three cars out of the lot, a small panel truck turned down the lane and disappeared.

"I wonder what's down there," I said.

"Don't know," said Eddie. "Why?"

"No reason."

Eddie just didn't seem to be the curious type, any more than the rest of Gogi's Gang. There wasn't much we needed to be curious about, really. We had our own tight little world with which we amused ourselves, a world full of rock, shopping, private comments that wouldn't mean much to anybody else, cars to take us wherever we wanted to go, and, of course, the Weary Why, which we felt was our own special club with one table that we always thought of as our own too. What more could anyone ask? I turned my face away from the dark little lane as we sped onto the expressway, with its endless ribbon of lights.

"Back in a second." Eddie pulled the car up to the yellow no-parking curb directly in front of the Discount Center.

I wanted to buy a battery for my transistor radio, but since Eddie seemed to be in such a hurry, I decided not to bother. I sat watching the people going in and out of the automatic doors, all in a rush because it must be nearly closing time. The uniformed guard on the exit door strolled back and forth, sometimes nodding to a departing customer but always watching everything. In the drug department, close to the door, a big fish-eye mirror glinted in the light, reflecting practically the whole store. Valencia was certainly getting citified, with mirrors to catch shoplifters and cameras that took people's pictures when they cashed checks at the supermarkets.

Eddie's blond head bobbed through the crowd down the long center aisle, and then he disappeared to the right in Men's Furnishings, out of range from where we were parked. I just hoped he wouldn't take a hundred years to decide on something. By the time we got back to Gogi's and then on to wherever we were going, I would have hardly any time left. Of course maybe nobody would know if I came in late. Mama and Mr. Duncan never stayed up much past eleven, and tonight, with the cookout, they might be tired enough to head for bed right away. Still, I could hardly count on it.

"OK. Let's go." Eddie, who must have come out of the farthest checkout counter, tossed a sack onto the back seat and whirled out of the parking space. "Got 'em. Also a couple of shirts."

I was surprised at that. This wasn't the kind of place where I would have expected him to buy his shirts—the Carnaby Shop, more likely, or Town and Country. In the side mirror I could see clusters of people hurrying out through the exits like ants leaving an anthill.

"Just in time" I said. "The place must be closing."

"Just made it." He spun around to the back of the store and down another dark street. "Shortcut."

"Don't worry," I said, reading the excuse about the shortcut loud and clear. "Nobody's going to catch you now."

"Huh?" His voice was startled.

"The trash cans," I said.

He turned to give me a long, searching look.

"That's right—the trash cans." His voice warmed. "You're a real cool kid, Cammy."

I glowed. I didn't know why I was a cool kid at just that

particular moment, but I didn't have to know. It was enough that he thought so. I was still dazed with joy as we walked into Gogi's, hand in hand.

"In here, Cammy." Gogi, in a brilliant green mini-bikini, ushered me impatiently down the hall to her bedroom, where Joellen and Sara were already dressed and waiting. "Dwight, show Eddie where to change." She shut the door and gestured toward half a dozen swimsuits tossed on the bed. "Take your pick."

"Oh, you bought the pink polka dot, after all!"

"It's my very own." Gogi tossed me the suit. "Wear it, then, and hurry."

I slid into the bikini, which Mama would definitely not have approved of, and put my own clothes into my tote bag.

"Bring the transistor," Gogi told Joellen. "Dwight's getting some stuff out of the freezer—refreshments yet." Her smile was triumphant. "Part of my mother's party food. It ought to thaw out just right by the time we need it."

Eddie, in black-and-yellow striped trunks, was coming down the hall toward the kitchen just as the girls all left Gogi's room.

"Sharp!" said Gogi. "Get a good deal on them?"

"The best," Eddie said lazily. "I got to try 'em on and all."

"Clever." I didn't know what was so clever about trying on something you were going to buy, but maybe Gogi only meant that the trunks were clever—another word that she had adopted just lately. "Consider your dues paid."

That must be another new phrase that meant something besides what it said. There were still a lot of expressions that Gogi's Gang used that I didn't quite fathom.

"Could I wear one of your new shirts over my suit?" I asked Eddie.

After all, I couldn't ride around in just a bikini.

"Out in the car."

"Oh, of course."

Naturally, he wouldn't have brought the shirts in—no sense to that.

"Everybody ready? Got the food hamper, Dwight?" Gogi flipped off the kitchen light. "We'll go out the back way." Unexpected car lights swept across the window and flared on the drive. "Oh, no! It's the parents, home already. Come on. Maybe we can make it out the front."

I stumbled over somebody as I tried to remember where the front door was.

"This way!" Gogi hissed, but it was too late.

A car door slammed, heels sounded on the tile of the utility room, and the kitchen switch clicked on. There was a little squeak of fright, and Gogi's mother—at least I took it for granted that it was Gogi's mother—said in a shaking voice, "What on earth is going on around here? You practically gave me a heart attack."

Six ✦✦✦✦✦

For a horrible moment, nobody said anything. We just stood there, looking as guilty as though we had been caught stealing the silver. Dwight, with his picnic hamper full of food, set it down hastily on the floor behind him.

"We—we—" For the first time since I had known Gogi, she seemed at a loss for words. "We were going swimming."

Mrs. Blakewood looked puzzled, as well she might, but she managed to sound hospitable.

"Oh, how nice! Daddy just had the pool cleaned today, all ready for our party tomorrow and— You jump right in now and have your swim, and I'll fix some sandwiches and—" She caught sight of me. "What a darling bikini!"

"Yes, I—" I was stammering right along with Gogi. "Isn't it, though?"

"I just wish Gogi could find one like it."

I looked at her with my mouth slightly ajar. Didn't she recognize her own daughter's clothes?

"Here comes Daddy." Mrs. Blakewood sounded as though she were glad of it. "Shoo now, all of you! I'll turn on his TV program and change my clothes and bring you all a bite to eat." Her eyes fell on the hamper on the floor. "What's in there?"

"Th-that?" Dwight looked as though he had never seen it before.

I gave a hysterical giggle and received a black look from Gogi, but even she couldn't think of a quick answer to that one. She resorted to irritability instead.

"Oh, Mama, never mind! It's just some stuff I have to put away. Go on and change your clothes, *please!*" She rolled her eyes in our direction. "Swim, y'all! I'll be right with you."

We obediently filed out, practically stepping on each others' heels. Looking back, like whoever it was that was turned to salt, I could see Gogi, with a furious expression, slamming the party food back into the freezer.

"A few less lights would help," Eddie muttered under the glare of the overhead floods. "Recreation hour in the prison yard."

"Better not make a break for it," I said out of the corner of my mouth. "Guards with shotguns on the wall, d'you think?"

"Yuh." He dabbled a toe in the water, uncertain what to do next. "Do we have to wait for Gogi?"

"She said to swim," I said, "so let's do it."

Eddie might feel like a convict, but I felt like an actress onstage, with any number of beady-eyed people looking at me from the other side of the footlights. I let myself quietly down into the pool, with Sara and Joellen alongside. Only Eddie dived in, and even he made only a small splash. We all paddled silently through the floodlit water, tinted a gorgeous blue from the aquamarine tiles lining the pool.

"My mother says don't make too much noise." Gogi finally arrived, looking like a thundercloud about to blast the earth with a bolt of lightning. "Neighbors."

Surely the neighbors didn't all go to bed at dusk, especially on a Saturday night. Probably they were having parties of their own, like Mama and Mr. D., or else they were out wherever older people went, maybe at a sedate copy of the Weary Why, with schmaltzy elderly music like "When Day Is Done" or "Dardanella."

We swam around for a while, up and down the pool, not saying much because nobody could think of anything to say, even in a quiet voice. Altogether, as a party this wasn't so great, and as just a swim it wasn't either. Pretty soon Mrs. Blakewood came out with a big tray of sandwiches—nothing like the fancy ones Gogi had almost made off with, I felt sure—and some soft drinks, which she set down on the concrete picnic table.

"Just help yourselves," she said with an anxious look at Gogi. "I hope you like ham salad. I didn't expect—"

"It's OK," said Gogi, making clear that it really wasn't.

"Looks good," I said cheerily.

I hated ham salad myself—not Mrs. Blakewood's fault, of course—but it was reasonable to suppose it would look good to anybody who liked it. Smiling determinedly, I took a sandwich, just for manners, and a can of ginger ale. I could always hide the sandwich in the shrubbery if I couldn't manage to get it down.

"Let's blow," Eddie muttered in my ear after another few minutes.

"Let's." I barely managed to stifle a yawn. I turned to Gogi, who was glowering at the sandwich tray. "We'll have to go now." I added the automatic words of thanks. "It was lovely, just lovely."

"Tell it like it is," Gogi snapped. "It was a frost." She

scowled. "Another five minutes and we'd really have been having fun out at Judge Hammond's place. They're gone for the weekend, it said in the paper."

"Win a few, lose a few," I said. "I'll just run in and change out of your bikini."

"Don't bother. You can wear it home."

"But—"

"In fact, you can keep it. Present. Free." Gogi sounded practically hysterical. "Lots more where that came from."

I didn't doubt that. All it took was money.

"Well, thanks, but—"

When Gogi was in a better mood, I would return the suit, saying that Mama wouldn't let me keep it, which she wouldn't if she knew anything about it. Maybe, though, she wouldn't even have to see it if I could get into the house unnoticed.

Everybody else except Dwight decided to leave, too, and we all swarmed out to our cars, relieved to be going. We called loud good-bys to each other—and never mind the presumably sleeping neighbors. Our three cars scratched off in close formation down the quiet street, one behind the other, like racers following the pace car on a speedway.

Eddie and I were last in line, tailgating Joellen and Mac, the way the driving instructor at school said never to do. But why worry? Eddie hadn't smashed up any cars yet.

"Do you still want to borrow one of my shirts?" asked Eddie.

Of course I did. It wasn't an especially cool night, but I was shivering a little in the damp bikini. I reached over into the back seat for the package and hauled it up front. The register receipt was still stapled to the mouth of the sack to make sure nobody walked out with anything that wasn't paid for, just another example of how suspicious people could be. I pulled the receipt loose and tossed it on the seat between us.

"Take your choice," said Eddie. "Plaid or white."

"White," I said.

With pink polka dots, plaid was impossible, even just to ride across town—especially this plaid, which was almost as wild as the one I had picked out for Jay. I couldn't imagine Eddie, always so smartly dressed, wearing a shirt like this, but maybe he had been in such a rush that he hadn't realized quite how hideous it was. I pulled out the plain white one, removed a dozen pins before putting it on, and laid the sack back on the rear seat.

"That's better," I said, ready to enjoy the night breeze now.

It would have been heavenly to keep on going forever, riding in close formation with these people who, such a little while ago, might as well have lived on another planet as far as I was concerned.

"She goes around with Gogi Blakewood," I heard somebody whispering behind me in the hall at school one day, "and dates Eddie Arden."

I hadn't even bothered to turn around and look but had simply walked on, cool and aloof, the way Gogi always was. I owed a lot of this, I felt sure, to the $39.95 dress, which had called me to her attention in the first place. I was still surprised that in spite of my poor start at the Weary Why that first evening, I had managed to grope my way along until I had made a place for myself. I wasn't sure just how— copying Gogi's way of acting and talking, maybe. Whatever the reason, I intended to keep on exactly as I had been. When something worked perfectly, it would be silly to change it in the slightest detail. Mama had always said I was a chameleon, hadn't she? And that was what chameleons did, matching themselves to their surroundings. Of course Mama had really been talking about all the projects that I took up and sometimes abandoned, not to any changes in my personality.

"Once a chameleon, always a chameleon," I murmured.

"H'm?" said Eddie.

"Nothing, actually."

I almost wished that we could go back to the Weary Why and pick up the evening where we had left off, but of course we weren't dressed for it now. Besides, it must be getting late. I didn't know how late because my watch was in the depths of my tote bag with my clothes. With a bleat of horns, Mac peeled off to the left toward Joellen's, Sara and Randy headed right, and Eddie and I were left alone, last in the formation.

"We'll stop and scrub the mascara off the license plate," he announced.

I thought it would be better to leave it the way it was until he got home, but maybe his father was the type who skulked around the garage reading license numbers and asking questions. A father or a cop—which was more dangerous? Again Eddie pulled up on a quiet street of darkened houses.

"What we need is cleansing cream." I dabbed in vain at the license plate with a piece of tissue. After all, mascara was advertised as being waterproof and almost everything-else-proof. "Maybe I could—" I rummaged in the bottomless tote bag and brought up my Pale Dream lipstick, which didn't match the numbers, of course, but might get by at night. "I'll dab some of this on so the sevens look sevenish again, but tomorrow you'd better try gasoline."

"Gee, thanks."

He was back to his old sardonic tone, which always made

me examine every word I had said to wonder whether it had been the right one. Maybe this time I had been a little too efficient with my advice about gasoline, which he was probably smart enough to think of for himself. The mother image was just what I wanted to avoid, especially since he didn't seem to be on very good terms with his parents, or anyway with his father. At least his father was right there in the same house, even if he did give Eddie some trouble. Mine didn't cause any trouble, but he might as well not even exist as far as his touching my life was concerned.

"Want a burger?" Eddie asked.

I shook my head.

"No, thanks. I have to be getting home."

I had hoped our house would be dark, but the lights were on in the living room, and the minute we drove up, the porch light snapped on, too.

"Uh-oh!" said Eddie. "Somebody's waiting up for you." He reached across me to open the door on my side. "Want me to come in with you?"

"No. Better not." There was no telling what Mama might say to him if, as I feared, we were really late. "See you around."

As I scrambled out of the car, a breeze caught the sales slip from the Discount Center and whirled it up the drive. I automatically picked it up and dropped it into my tote bag to be tossed into the wastebasket later, because Mama never liked paper blowing around the yard.

"We've been concerned." It was not Mama but Mr. D., in robe and slippers, who was waiting for me in the hall.

I put on an air of surprise.

"Am I late?"

"It's one o'clock. I believe you told your mother you'd be in at twelve."

Mama, stern-faced, appeared in the hallway, too.

"Besides not having permission to go in the first place," she added.

I hastened to get off that particular section of dangerous ground.

"I didn't mean to be late," I said. "I went swimming at Gogi's and then we had car trouble and—" Changing the numbers on the license plate and then changing them back again could be classified as car trouble, and so could tipping over the trash cans, if I wanted to stretch a point, as I certainly did just then. "So the time just went."

Mama suddenly noticed my costume.

"What on earth do you have on?"

I hugged Eddie's shirt around me to make sure she didn't get much of a look.

"One of Gogi's suits. I didn't take time to change because — Well, you said yourself I was late."

"Next time you're late, which I hope won't be soon, I suggest that you telephone," Mr. Duncan put in, very teacherish. "That's not unreasonable, is it?"

"No, sir."

Not a word about his being upset himself, further proof of how little I really mattered to him. Never a thought about how I might feel myself. Had he ever wondered for even a minute whether I might be upset by his pushing me out of my secure place in Mama's life? Of course he hadn't. It was just Mama he was fretting about. He looked at my stormy face.

"I feel responsible for you, too, Cammy," he said in a gentler voice. "Run on to bed now, and we'll talk about this some more tomorrow."

Not if I could help it, we wouldn't. I didn't see what there was to discuss, anyway. I had been late. I had worried

Mama. I mustn't do it again, as I would certainly try not to. It would be simply too horrible if Eddie were ever trapped in one of these sessions. It was so lucky that he had left right away instead of taking me to the door.

"Good night, then," I said with chilly politeness. "So sorry."

I hurried down the hall to my room and locked the door, just in case Mama might tag along and get a good look at Gogi's bikini, which was definitely on the startling side, even to me. I scrambled into my shortie pajamas and stuck the bikini up on my closet shelf behind the train case that I wouldn't be taking down for a good long while unless I got an unexpected invitation to New York, which at this moment seemed about as unlikely as finding a diamond mine in the back yard.

Luckily the spotlight veered away from me the next morning because the police called Mr. Duncan to go out to school on account of some vandals having broken in and smashed a lot of windows and poured molasses into the office typewriters. In the face of that, Mama didn't say a word about a minor thing like my being an hour late getting in from my date.

"I just can't understand," she said, "what satisfaction anybody gets from breaking things up like that. It's so senseless."

I sometimes felt like smashing things myself as a way of rebelling against whatever I didn't like in the world, but I certainly wasn't going to say so. I was already in enough disfavor for last night's episode.

"I'm going to hit the books," I said virtuously.

That ought to get me off the hook with both Mama and Mr. D., who naturally esteemed study. I didn't have anything to do all day, anyway. Besides, I really was a long way behind, much farther than I had realized. I owed a book report in English, besides not having even picked the subject for my term paper. It was plenty early to start work on that, but it would be nice to have a running start, like Jay, and Katy, too, probably. She had always been a great one for doing her work well ahead, a real all-right kid, at least from the teachers' standpoint.

"There's Katy, going by with Brandy," Mama called. "I'll just run out and ask her to come in."

"I'm *studying*," I wailed, but it was too late.

Mama was out, Katy was in, and Brandy, looking reproachful was leashed to the grapefruit tree just outside my window.

"Well, hi!" Katy stood hesitantly in the doorway to my room as though she thought it might be booby-trapped. "Doing homework?"

I nodded, trying to look busy enough so she would go away. I didn't like feeling the way I felt now in Katy's presence, as though I had just picked up a dog by the ears or hidden the baby's bottle. It wasn't that Katy looked downtrodden, not in the least. On the contrary, she had never looked better. She had shed a few pounds and was wearing her hair short and curly, for a change. She was definitely nervous, though, and so was I, because after a moment of awkward silence we both began talking at once, breaking in on each other's sentences before we could finish them.

"I hear you're running for—" I began.

"Jay told me you— Oh, excuse me. Yes. I am. It's—"

"Oh, I know it's fun. I hope you—"

"I wish you could have stopped by and—"

"Oh, I'm so terrible at posters. I always—"

"You are not! Don't you remember the ones you—"

I didn't want to remember anything, so I kept yakking

away as though there were a prize for whoever could crash through with the most words.

"I had a date. Swimming at—"

Come to think about it, I didn't know why Gogi was so fired up about swimming all of a sudden. She was definitely not the athletic type, but if I had as many bikinis as she had, I would certainly try for a chance to show them off. Maybe giving them away—had she presented Sara and Joellen with the ones they had borrowed, too?—served the same purpose, making her look like the little rich girl tossing gifts to the lower classes. That was a hateful thought, which I hastily rejected. Gogi was naturally generous. Look at the lipsticks and the mascara and all the other little goodies that she was forever passing out to her friends. I let my glance stray to my pile of books, and Katy got the message.

"I have to go," she said. "Brandy'll have that tree pulled up by the roots."

Without even thinking about it, I got up to walk her halfway home—a programmed robot doing automatically what I had done practically all my life. Brandy, delighted to see me, plunged at the end of his leash, and the grapefruit tree quivered.

"He remembers you," said Katy. "Every time we go by, he tries to—" The words died on her lips. "All right, Brandy. Cool it."

She unwound him from the tree, and he lumbered over to me, plumy tail waving.

"Good Brandy." I repeated the old familiar words. "He's a good boy."

Pleased with praise, he put his paws on my shoulders and gazed into my eyes. I staggered out from under as Katy tugged on the leash.

"No, Brandy! Sit!" she ordered. Brandy immediately

rolled over and played dead. "He never did understand English."

"Oh, he understands, all right. He just wants to do as he pleases. Does he still—"

So I was at it, too, raking up things from the past. I gave the recumbent Brandy a final pat, said, "Hope you get elected," to Katy and turned back toward the house.

"Oh, I forgot to tell you—" Katy began, but then she decided to forget it permanently and went on down the street with Brandy.

That "Oh, I forgot to tell you" stayed in my mind all day long, a reminder of the times when Katy and I had chattered endlessly, never at a loss for things to talk about, from mystery stories to the way to get the ticks off Brandy. It wouldn't be hard to slip back into the old easy friendship in case I ever wanted to, but for now, being friends with Gogi's Gang took up all my time. Besides, Katy must have a whole swarm of new friends by now—Jay, for instance, and probably lots of others that I didn't even know about.

I studied all the rest of the day—or at least held books in front of my face—stopping only for dinner, which I dreaded because Mama and/or Mr. D. might start harping on last night again.

"Homework going all right?" Mr. D. inquired. "Your mother says you've been at it all day."

One gold star for me! And maybe one for Mama, too, for letting him know I had been working.

"Oh, sure. All OK."

That was an exaggeration, to say the least. I had read a lot of words, but I doubted if many of them had soaked in. Instead, my mind had gone leaping from crag to crag like a mountain goat. I had thought about Eddie and Katy and Jay and Gogi and Mama and Mr. D. and even my father and Dina (unfavorably). Everything was so changed now from when I came home from New York. Whenever I was with Gogi's Gang, I felt like a glamorous stranger to myself. The rest of the time I was a confusing mixture—traces of the old me, enthusiastic, talkative, darting off in all directions, added to the new, sleeker "in" girl, sophisticated, at least on the surface, and carefully cool. It was a peculiar feeling as though I were standing off somewhere looking at myself from a distance.

The homework did the trick for me because Mama and Mr. D. talked around me during most of dinner, discussing the school situation instead of my crime against parental authority.

"A respite, at least," Mr. D. said, "but whether the legislature will do any better in the special session than they did before is hard to say. Same people, same ideas."

"Plus politics," said Mama.

"Which, let's face it, is always the determining factor in the end." He turned to me. "What do your friends think about all this?"

"Well—uh—nothing, actually." I floundered for words. "It's more for—uh—older people." I couldn't imagine Gogi, for instance, getting in a froth because the teachers were upset about whatever they were upset about. "Jay, though— But his mother's a teacher, so naturally—" I hastily abandoned that line of thought, which underlined the point that Mr. D. was an educator, too, so I might be expected to be as interested as Jay, or nearly. The fact that I wasn't was just more evidence that things weren't working out right at home. "I guess, really, I don't know exactly what it's all about."

"It's a fight between the legislature and the teachers, who are demanding more classrooms, fewer students, up-to-date textbooks and enough of them." He warmed to his subject. "I could go on and on—a statewide kindergarten program, better salaries so Florida can compete in attracting and keeping good teachers—" His shoulders sagged. "Try and get 'em, the way our tax structure is set up." He gave me a half-smile. "Pretty dull stuff for the young."

He was right about that, although I felt an unwilling quiver of sympathy. Older people seemed to worry just as much as the rest of us but about such unglamorous things, like tax structures and legislatures and textbooks. I fretted a good deal about my image with Gogi's Gang, my dates with Eddie, and what to wear to the Weary Why, but at least it was a more interesting type of worrying.

"You might listen around a little," Mama suggested. "It helps to know what other people are thinking."

"Oh, naturally." Tired of this kind of discussion, I pushed my chair back. "If you'll excuse me, I'll get back to my homework."

I sat fidgeting at my desk, getting up to investigate a strange sound (an acorn bouncing off the metal awning), sharpening an already sharp pencil and nobly emptying the shavings into the wastebasket, putting on fresh lipstick, riffling through my notebook for the history assignment, anything not to settle down to my books. I kept wishing Gogi would call, although she hardly ever did, preferring to announce her plans for the gang either at school or during a shopping trip. Anyway, her parents might insist on her attending their swimming party today, just as Mama had made me come to the cookout.

Up until last night, I had pictured Gogi as a completely free spirit, but now I had a different idea. When her mother arrived, Gogi had stayed right there in the home pool without a word of argument when I had expected her to erupt like Fourth of July fireworks. I smiled to myself. It was a comforting thought to know that even Gogi didn't have her parents under absolutely complete control, for all her doing exactly as she pleased most of the time.

Mama stuck her head in the door, and I stiffened. Here came the lecture, in spite of all my efforts to avoid it.

"Anything I can do to help?" she asked.

I gave her a suspicious look. Maybe this was just leading up to the scolding by an indirect route. Before she married Mr. D., she used to help me with my homework all the time, skimming through the book so she could ask me questions about it or checking over my themes to see whether I had made any mistakes in grammar or spelling. Now that I was a senior, though, it seemed kiddish to have my mother help me, as though I couldn't handle it myself. Besides, I didn't want her to find out how far behind I was.

"Oh, I'm doing fine," I said.

"You're sure?" She hesitated. "Then I believe Roger and I will run down to the Beckers' for a little bridge. Roger needs some relaxation, what with the break-in at school and—"

And waiting up for me until one o'clock—I knew the end to that sentence. I scowled. So all right. Let them go. Probably Mama wasn't really interested in my homework anyway but was only checking up to make sure I was doing what I said I was.

"You wouldn't feel you could spare the time to come, too?" she asked. "I know Katy'd be glad."

"Katy's busy, too," I said—not that we hadn't studied in chorus lots of times. "Besides, I have to type a theme."

I had to when it was written, which probably wouldn't be today, at the rate I was going. Mama, very motherly, patted my shoulder.

"All right then, if you're sure. We won't be late."

I didn't look up as she left, but I did stand at the window as she and Mr. D. strolled down the drive and headed for the Beckers'. As soon as they were out of sight, I dashed to the telephone and looked up Gogi's number. There was no law that I couldn't call her just to chat, and if it happened to remind her that it would be fun for us all to get together somewhere, that would be nice, too.

The telephone rang for a long time, and then an impatient male voice said, "Blakewoods'." Somewhere in the background, I heard a babble of conversation and the splash of water—the Blakewoods' swimming party in full swing, of course.

"Hello, hello," the voice said. "Speak up!"

Without saying a word, I carefully replaced the receiver.

Seven ❖❖❖❖❖

"Sad." Gogi, waiting in the hall for English class to begin, gave me a weary look. "Don't you have windows at your house?"

"Windows?"

"To climb out of."

"Ha! I'd never get away with it."

"Well, if you're not allowed out, I'll just have to round up somebody else for the Halloween Howl. I wonder who—"

"The Halloween Howl? What's that?"

"I haven't decided yet. A howl, that's all."

I couldn't imagine what she meant by that—something square, maybe, that she and the rest would make fun of behind their smooth noncommittal faces. Of course Gogi's Gang would never use the word square or even corny or hammy, which belonged with the outdated slang that Mama might use or maybe Mr. D. Uncool was probably the right word for whatever she had in mind.

"Maybe I could get Eddie a date with—" Gogi put on a thoughtful look.

"I didn't say I couldn't date at all," I said, panic-stricken.

"I just can't go out more than one night a week for a while."

It would have to be on a Friday or a Saturday, depending on when Eddie asked me to the Weary Why or wherever the gang might be going. Then on all the other nights while I sat at home studying madly, I could amuse myself by wondering which girl Eddie was taking out instead of me. A lot of good that kind of studying would do! I scowled. I was positive that this whole thing was another of Mr. Duncan's ideas, although it had been Mama who had broken the news.

"One date a week and home every afternoon by four-thirty, at least for the next six weeks," she had said sternly. "I never *saw* such a report card!"

I had to admit that it wasn't the greatest, but I hadn't actually failed in anything. I had rated an incomplete in English for this first six weeks because of the book review that I had never turned in, and a D and two C—'s in the other stuff. A C in phys. ed. was my best grade of all, since that class didn't require any homework or preparation. Besides, I had always been pretty fair on the parallel bars, having started at an early age on the jungle gym that Katy and I had shared.

"See you around," said Gogi as the bell rang and we went into class.

After the first week of school, the teacher had assigned her a seat as far from me as possible without even explaining why. She couldn't accuse us of talking in class, but probably she knew that she wasn't getting my undivided attention or Gogi's either.

I didn't like Gogi's "See you around," which sounded altogether too vague about the future. She hadn't even asked me to go shopping with her and Joellen today, but even if she had, there wouldn't have been time enough to cover very much ground between three-fifteen, when school let out, and my four-thirty deadline.

"I'm going to start hearing your lessons again the way I always used to." Mama's words set up an unpleasant echo in my mind. "And Roger will help you on the things I don't know so much about."

And wasn't that going to be the greatest thing since television! Probably Mr. D. couldn't stand having everybody know that I, his very own stepdaughter, was on the ragged edge of flunking—a horrible image for the principal of Citrus High School. In a way, it was funny, a good joke on Mr. D., except that I was the one who was getting the ax.

"It isn't that you're not smart." Mama sounded almost tearful. "You just don't study, now that you're going with this new crowd. Nothing like this ever happened when you and Katy were good friends."

Katy again! Couldn't anything happen without Katy's name being dragged in?

"We're still good friends," I mumbled.

That was exaggerating things a little, but at least we spoke when we met. All of a sudden, Katy was a big important somebody at school, now that she had won the election, due mostly, I thought, to Jay's lively campaigning, complete with banners, a parade, some soapbox oratory out in the parking lot during lunch hour, and Brandy, decked out with signs saying *Vote for Katy*. I had followed Brandy's advice although nobody else in Gogi's Gang had bothered even to cast a ballot.

"What for?" Gogi had demanded. "Who cares about stuff like that?"

"It's all so dull," Joellen, the faithful echo, had chimed in.

"Well, yes, but—"

I should have known better than to mention the election which was one of those things that practically everybody else in school got all fired up about but Gogi, naturally, didn't.

"Practice in politics," Mr. Duncan had said at dinner one night, "only with the unsavory parts omitted. At least I don't think anybody has been buying any votes." He threw me a sidewise smile. "Not to disillusion your young mind, of course."

My young mind was medium disillusioned already, although not with high school elections.

"Ride?" asked Katy as I waited for the city bus the day I had broken the news to Gogi about my being grounded for six weeks.

I nodded and climbed in, dumping my armload of books on the seat with Katy's collection. It had been a long time since I had had to think about getting a ride, by bus or otherwise, because nearly every afternoon after school I went to one of the shopping centers with Gogi and Joellen, who, of course, took me home afterward. Today I had a horrible suspicion that Gogi was out hunting somebody to take my place in the gang any time I couldn't show up whenever she wanted me.

"Congratulations," I said, not having seen Katy since the election.

"Oh, thanks," she said in an offhand voice. "Lots of work, I guess, but somebody has to do it."

I wasn't really sure what kind of work it was, but I wouldn't dream of asking.

"Jay did a good job on your campaign," I went on.

Being one of Gogi's Gang, I should be feeling superior to Katy and her doings, but instead, for some reason, I was anxious to show her that I knew what was going on.

"Jay's a sharp kid," Katy agreed. "I just wish—" She hesitated and changed the subject, so I never did find out what she wished. "How about making a batch of posters for the Halloween dance?"

"Me? Oh, no, I couldn't. I—I don't have that night free."

I didn't even know which night it was going to be, but I certainly wouldn't take any chances on missing Gogi's Halloween Howl, whatever and whenever it was.

"You don't have to make them the night of the dance," said Katy with a little snap in her voice. "I need them next Tuesday." She didn't wait for me to think up any more excuses. "It'll be such a help, and thank you very much. Ten will be enough, if they're fairly big. Just reach in the front of my notebook, and you'll find all the dope about where and when and how much."

I didn't remember that Katy had been so efficient before or so bossy either. Still, I wouldn't actually mind doing the posters. It might be fun, in fact, if I could work them in with all the homework.

"If Mama will let me, OK," I said feebly. "She—they— I didn't get such a good report card."

"Oh, you can manage a few posters. You were always faster than lightning on things like that."

Flattery, flattery, except that it was in the past tense. It was true, though, that I used to be able to whip up posters and place cards and invitations with no trouble at all. Now that I hadn't for a while, I decided that maybe I even missed my projects just a little. Besides, with all those hours at home, I was going to need something to do besides schoolwork.

"Get whatever material you need," said Katy, "and the Student Council will pay you back, OK?"

"Oh, sure." Already I was thinking about cutout pumpkin heads and ghosts and witches. "What's the music?"

"The Devil's Own."

"Great! I can—" But I decided not to tell her what I had in mind until I could get it worked out to suit me. I glanced at my watch. "Would you have time to stop by the Art Shop? If we hurry, we can just about make it."

"Oh, I have lots of time."

"Yes, but I don't. I have to be home by four-thirty." My voice shook. "Every school day, and only one night out a week."

Katy made a noncommittal sound that I didn't try to translate. She certainly didn't offer any sympathy or ask even one question, but probably, having all her faculties, she had figured out that it was my report card that was keeping me grounded. I wished now that I hadn't said even as much as I had. Katy was never in trouble with her parents—that I knew of, anyway—and she wouldn't be able to understand my letting my homework slide just to run around the town with Gogi and her crowd. Poor Katy! She simply didn't realize how lovely it was to sit at the Weary Why, drifting with the music and the shifting lights, with nothing at all on my mind except the here and the now and the feeling of belonging in this special place with all my friends.

"I'll get on it as soon as I can," I told Katy when she dropped me off at home with an armload of poster paper and some jars of paint. "And thanks for the ride."

It had been rather an expensive ride from my point of view because I had been practically shanghaied into doing something that I really didn't want to do. Or maybe I only meant that it was something that Gogi wouldn't want to do, and since I was trying to be as much like Gogi as possible, I naturally tried to think as she thought. I sighed. I was doing altogether too much thinking lately about my own thought processes and about a lot of other things besides.

I stacked my books on my desk and rooted around in my tote bag for my Pale Dream lipstick, which was getting a little stubby now, to see whether it might be good for a few more days. As usual when I was trying to find something, I dredged up a lot of other things first from the assortment of debris that always settled to the bottom—three bobby pins, a paper clip, a cafeteria napkin, half a stick of gum, and Eddie's sales slip from the Discount Center which I had forgotten to throw away. Maybe I would keep it, though, for the scrapbook I was going to bring up to date the first chance I got—or maybe the second. I glanced at the slip—$2.25, $2.25, Total $4.50, plus tax, cheap enough for two shirts and a pair of swim trunks. Maybe though, there had been a separate slip for the trunks. I tossed the receipt into my bottom desk drawer.

"Cammy?" Mama called from the kitchen. "Couldn't Katy come in?"

"I didn't ask her," I called back. "I have to study, don't I?"

There was a moment of silence.

"Yes," Mama said in a level voice, "you do."

Studying was what I did from then on, day after day, night after night until I was ready to scream.

"Name the plot sources for *Macbeth*," Mama would say, or, "Was Lady Macbeth a stronger personality than her husband?"

"You should have been a teacher," I would remark crossly, but under Mama's guidance I did know most of the answers on our pop quiz, and I did turn in my book review on time, besides catching up on the one I hadn't done the first six weeks. I even picked out the topic for my term paper in English, "Science Fiction and Its Place in American Literature," a subject that sounded suitably intellectual.

"I had to pick something," I told Mama, "and that was about all that was left on the list."

At least, it was the only one that wasn't on an even harder subject. Because I was starting to do my reading for it, I was allowed to go to the public library in the evening to look up references. Mama probably figured, accurately, too, that nobody in Gogi's Gang would be there to distract me. I came home loaded with books by Andre Norton, Robert Heinlein, and Isaac Azimov and grew accustomed to threading my way through the galaxies aboard spaceships or stepping forward in time a thousand years or so. Outlandish vegetation, mutants with uncanny powers, infra-scopes and beamers—at least they took my mind off my annoyance at being kept in and my always lurking worry about whether somebody else might be going to take my place in Gogi's Gang.

"Ready for U.S. History?" Mr. D. came wandering into the dining room, where Mama and I were still discussing Shakespeare. He picked up one of my science-fiction books. "Heinlein, h'm? One of the early ones in the field." He flipped the pages. "I always did go for science fiction."

I felt a flicker of surprise. Who would have supposed that Mr. D. would be interested in anything as remote from school as these explorers of unknown worlds? Probably, though, he was just talking that way to give me the impression that he shared my interests.

"They're OK," I said haughtily. "Different, if nothing else."

Mama closed the literature book with a snap.

"Why, Cammy Chase! You said just yesterday that you were absolutely fascinated—and I quote!"

Mr. D. gave me a long look, and his lips twitched.

"There's no more healthful exercise than jumping from one side of the fence to the other," he said lightly, "especially to get away from somebody."

I blushed angrily. My remark about science fiction had been purely contrary—automatic opposition to Mr. D.'s opinion—but it was unsettling to have him read my motives as clearly as though I had explained them to him in complete detail.

"Run along to your meeting, Marian," he told Mama. "Cammy and I have to fight our way through the American Revolution tonight."

From the glint in his eye, I suspected that the Revolution wasn't the only thing we were going to fight through, but he started mildly enough with a question about the causes of the war.

"Taxation without representation," I parroted from the pages that I had read just that afternoon. "The desire for freedom from the mother country."

"Exactly," he said. "Even countries want to cut the apron strings. Do you see a possible parallel here between a young country and the young people of today, all anxious to run their own affairs?"

So here came the lecture, although I wasn't sure quite what direction it was going to take.

"Well, the colonists were mad at England because they couldn't do as they pleased. Same for people, too, I guess."

"Hostility then, but based on what, do you think?"

I knew the answer to that one.

"Rebellion against authority," I said smartly. "Isn't that what all the parents keep screaming about?"

"It's what the youngsters keep screaming about, anyway." His voice continued calm. "Why do you think England felt she had a right to authority over the colony?"

"For England, read parents?" I inquired.

"If you like," he said.

"Well, they probably think they know more."

"True. Countries *or* parents."

I abandoned England entirely.

"And I guess they love us," I said, reluctantly honest, "in their own way."

"I guess they do," Mr. D. agreed, "even though you make it rough sometimes." His voice hardened. "Especially for stepparents."

I carefully avoided his eyes. I didn't want to be reminded that he was probably trying to be a father to me, although naturally not so much on my own account as because I was Mama's daughter and he was stuck with me.

"It would be a sorry pair of parents that would turn a child loose in the world before she had acquired the necessary weapons to protect herself," he said. "You have to learn to use freedom."

I stifled a yawn.

"In the case of the colonies," I said, scurrying back onto safe ground, "I believe they were fully qualified for freedom."

"Quite right. They were. The country was young but not too young to have acquired experience and survived hardship. Now, do you want to give me a quick rundown on some of the highlights of the early part of the Revolution?"

I didn't think there was any trap here, so I chattered along about the Boston Tea Party, Paul Revere's Ride, and whatever else I could think of.

"Excellent," Mr. D. said. "I think you have this all well

in mind." He pushed back his chair. "I'll leave you to your math, then." He picked up *Dark Piper*. "If you're not using this right now for your paper, may I borrow it? I'm a little behind on the doings among the planets."

"You'll like it," I said, forgetting my earlier pose of indifference. "Very exciting." I hesitated. "And thank you for your help."

Probably he thought I was thanking him for his explanation of how parents felt about freedom for their children. Actually I was only being polite about his tutoring, which I had to admit was always helpful in bringing out the reasons behind the facts of history. He must have been a good teacher before he became a principal, but he hadn't quite gotten the message about my hostility toward him. It wasn't really freedom I was fussing about. After all, I did have a life of my own with Gogi's Gang—so far, at least. The truth was, I was just plain jealous because Mr. D. had replaced me as the center of Mama's life. What I wanted was for everything to be just as it always had been, frozen in time, so that I would have a familiar place to retreat to in case I needed it. In the back of my mind, I realized that this might be an unrealistic wish, but I clung to it stubbornly. Somebody had to be to blame for all the changes at home, and Mr. D. was the only candidate I could think of.

"Something else." He stuck his head back into the dining room. "Just remember that if you can stand the—uh—situation just a few more months, you'll be away at college. Everything changes then."

"Uh-huh." I kept my head bent studiously over my math book.

Just a few more months! About ten—so near a year that it didn't matter. If this was his idea of consolation, it wasn't much, at least for me. It would be for him, though, when I went off to college and left him in complete possession. Anyway, now was when I wanted things the way I wanted them, not next year.

"When your mother and you decide what college you want," Mr. D. offered, "I'll help you make out the application. The sooner the better, the way things are."

The way things were was that it was rough getting into a good college without terrific grades, which I didn't have. They would doubtless improve, now that I didn't do much except study, but even so the overall average would be only medium, maybe C+ or B— if I was especially lucky.

Getting into college was a subject that Katy and I used to talk about a lot—another thing that Gogi's Gang ignored. From what they said, I would never suspect that they even intended to go to college, although I supposed they did, the boys to postpone the draft, if for nothing else, and the girls just because that was what people did. I felt a little quiver of excitement. Tomorrow I would try to find out where Gogi and Joellen and Sara were going and see if I could go there, too. Maybe I could even room with one of them. Katy and I had always planned to room together, but of course that was out now.

"Wouldn't it be great," I might say to Gogi, "if we could all go the same place to college? Gogi's Gang, Florida State division."

The trouble was, it would be hard to get up my courage to say it. As leader of the gang, Gogi preferred to arrange things herself, but maybe I could find a way of hinting around without actually making the suggestion myself.

"I simply can't decide," I might say. "I have to get my application in pretty soon, and—"

Here there would be a pause, which I hoped would be filled by some remark like, "Oh, we're all going to Gainesville (or Miami or Florida Southern), so why don't you put in there, too?"

On the other hand, that might not be what Gogi would say at all. The silence might just lengthen until somebody said, "Oh, maybe we'll go to modeling school" —not that I could imagine their being even remotely interested in anything like that either.

All the way to school with Mr. D. the next morning, I tried to build up my courage to introduce the subject to Gogi. It was so very, very important that everything should go just right. Katy hailed me as I was trudging gloomily up the steps of the auditorium.

"We put your posters up yesterday, did you see? They look really great."

I had turned them over to her over the weekend—an assortment of witches with huge paper flowers in their teeth, black cats shadowed by ghostly white kittens, skeletons grinning horribly, and fiery devils clutching guitars marked "The Devil's Own."

The posters proclaimed:

STUDENT COUNCIL HALLOWEEN MASQUERADE DANCE,
GYM, SATURDAY, *9* TO *1*

"Nobody's going to want to miss it," said Katy. "Those posters really stand out."

I thought they were pretty sharp myself—big and bright and lively and fun to do, besides.

"I hope you can come, after all," said Katy. She carefully avoided my eye. "If you don't have a— I mean, if Eddie can't make it, I can get you a date. I know somebody who—"

"Who?" I asked.

"Well, Jay would be glad to—"

"But I thought—" What was going on here? I had supposed that Jay would be going with Katy, who else? Or was this the big sacrificial gesture—giving up her own date for me? "I can't come, anyway. I told you. But thank you just the same."

Katy waved a negligent hand.

"If your plans change—"

I didn't really have any plans, but I always left Saturday nights free for Eddie to take me to the Weary Why, which so far he had never failed to do.

"My plans won't change," I said.

Famous last words, because as I scuttled into English class past one of my posters showing a skeleton wearing a pirate's mask and brandishing a cutlass, Gogi jerked a finger toward the picture.

"That'll be it!" she said. "The Halloween Howl. I can see it all now. We'll go in our dear sweet little costumes and bob for apples and—"

She paused for breath, and Joellen picked up the chant.

"And shake hands with a glove full of wet sand and—"

"And dance the Virginia Reel, probably," Sara chimed in. "How absolutely *ridiculous* can you get?"

Eight ✣✣✣✣✣

"Dance?"

A large spotted dog with a face like Brandy's and a keg marked *XXX* dangling around his neck held out an inviting paw as I sat with Gogi's Gang at the table where we had settled ourselves for the dance. In the center of the Halloween cloth, a jack-o'-lantern grinned at a room festooned with orange and black crepe paper and at cornstalks interspersed with ghosts and plywood witches. On the portable stage, the Devil's Own were giving forth with rock for a crowd of costumed dancers.

"See?" Gogi had said, arriving. "Isn't it an absolute howl? I could tell from those silly posters."

I gave her a narrow look from behind my mask. Probably she didn't know that I was the one who had made the posters—I hadn't signed them, naturally—but just the same I couldn't help feeling wounded. For a Halloween dance you had to have Halloween posters, didn't you? And I hadn't seen any of the childish games, like bobbing for apples, that Gogi had anticipated. Obviously, though, she thought that Halloween as a whole was just too tiresome, although in some peculiar way she seemed to get a kick out of her own boredom.

"Dance?" the dog repeated, getting down on his hind legs and holding up his front paws as though he were begging.

"Well, I—"

None of Gogi's Gang were dancing. They hardly ever did, even at the Weary Why. Instead, they were just sitting there, making snide remarks about the whole affair.

"Oh, go *on!*" Gogi said in a tired voice. "Halloween comes but once a year, I always say."

I got up, glittering in the satin spacewoman's outfit that I had copied out of one of the science-fiction books I was reading for my senior theme. Antennae to pick up the vibrations from outer space quivered on top of my head, and a make-believe laser rod hung from my wide belt. I had been terribly proud of coming up with something really unique and far-out until I had seen that nobody in the gang had tried for anything more complex than a ghostly sheet, a clown suit, or a pirate outfit straight out of the dime store. "Why bother?" Gogi had probably said.

When I had emerged from the house in my shining costume, Gogi, who was in a babyish mini-skirt with a big bow in her hair, had flung me a bored glance.

"Trying to win first prize or something?"

I was sure that she would think winning a prize at a masquerade was absolutely childish, but the prize wasn't at all what I had had in mind. I had simply wanted to be a credit to my friends, and copying a costume from a description in one of the science-fiction books had seemed like a real inspiration. It was just another example of how different Gogi's view of things was from most people's. Probably she thought that dancing with this St. Bernard dog was kid stuff, too, but she had said to go ahead, hadn't she? Besides,

Eddie wasn't even here yet, so I felt like a fifth wheel.

"Dwight and Gogi'll pick you up," he had told me over the telephone. "Big blast at the base, and the old man says I have to show. See you at the gym around ten-thirty maybe."

That "maybe" sounded altogether too uncertain, but if Eddie's parents had him cornered, there was probably nothing he could do about it. I let the St. Bernard nudge me out onto the floor. I didn't even care very much who it was, although the fact that he had picked me out of the middle of Gogi's Gang was a sign that he was somebody who wasn't quite with it. A boy didn't ask to dance with somebody else's date, no matter what Mama had to say about how tiresome it must be to stick with the same person all evening. Of course, my date wasn't visible just then. Not only that, how did this St. Bernard even know who I was in the first place? Probably, in fact, he didn't.

"Who are you?" I demanded as we plowed out onto the floor for the Mexican Hat Dance, which wasn't exactly the latest thing but at least wasn't as historical as the Virginia Reel that Gogi had expected.

"I'm a noble St. Bernard." The keg around his neck banged on his chest as he danced. "Specializing in rescuing stranded maidens."

"Rescuing them from what?" He must have himself confused with a knight of the Round Table.

"From boredom. You didn't look as though you were having a real great time."

How could he tell what kind of time I was having with my face hidden behind a mask?

"Oh, I was! The greatest." I could have used a breath of air, though. I was simmering in my space outfit, and my fur-covered partner must be even warmer. "Who do you think I am, anyway?"

"The 'in' girl, who else?" His voice reverberated behind the dog mask. "Newest member of Gogi's Gang. How lucky can you get?"

I stopped dead in my tracks.

"Now, listen, Jay Vernon, if you're going to be hateful, I don't have to—"

"Hateful? Me? You mean you aren't the 'in' girl? You don't feel lucky?"

His dog ears flapped as he lumbered through the Hat Dance.

"Oh, of course I am! I mean, I do." I was tempted to plant a boot heel on one of his furry paws. "And even if I wasn't, what's it *to* you?"

"A good question." His voice turned serious or sincere or something in that general area. "Maybe I just want to tell you to watch it." He waved a paw in the direction of Gogi's Gang. "Not your kind of people, kid."

"They are *so* my kind of people. They—" I was glad I had my mask on because I could feel tears of anger welling up. "Oh, you're just jealous."

His blue eyes glittered through the holes in his mask.

"You could be right."

"I can't help it if they don't ask you into the gang, can I?" I raged.

"Nope," he agreed. "Where'd you get the idea I wanted to be asked in?"

"But you said—"

"Sure. I said I was jealous, or you said it, or somebody." A brief pause. "I've got news for you. There's more than one kind of jealous."

"If you're going to get philosophical," I said, bewildered, "this isn't the place."

"Right. Maybe it's something about the masks. You talk through them, and it isn't really you. Gives you a good out. You can always pretend afterward it was somebody else that said it." He shrugged. "Want to step outside?"

"And fight?"

"And cool off."

I stole a look at Gogi's Gang, still staring through their masks, but evidently not at me. Eddie was still absent.

"All right," I said. "Just for a minute."

He stopped at the machine and got a couple of colas on the way out. We cut across the parking lot and sat down on a stone bench marked *Gift of Class of 1962*. Jay lifted off the dog head and put it down beside him. I tilted up my own mask and gulped fresh air.

"Where's Katy?" I asked. "I thought you'd be coming with her."

"She's taking tickets."

He answered one part of my question but not the other. I let the silence drag on for a couple of minutes. Maybe he really had something with his idea about the effect of wearing masks. Certainly there had been no awkward silences when we had had them on a couple of minutes ago. I had better think of something to talk about right away before he resumed his lecturing. I seized on the first subject that I could think of.

"Where do you live?" I asked. "I never did know."

"Did you ever notice that sand road beside the Weary Why? Our house is down at the end of it on a little lake. My grandfather left it to Mom."

"The field with the horses, too?"

I could shut my eyes and see them standing there in the

shade of the big water oaks, peering curiously toward the Weary Why with its jangle of electronic music. Jay nodded.

"They're getting old, but I ride them when I have time—not often—and Mom even wrote some music about them once."

"Music?"

It had never occurred to me that people who taught music might actually be composers when they were at home.

"Oh, sure. She's good, too. She wrote one number for the school chorus that's real solid."

I looked at him curiously—and almost enviously. He actually spoke of his mother as though she were an individual, not just one of a large enemy group all more or less alike. Not only that, he sounded really truly interested in what she was doing—which was definitely not according to the current rules concerning parents. Of course he didn't have a stepfather to contend with. I had gotten along fine with my own mother before Mr. Duncan stepped into the picture. We had even had fun, but that was last year, a long time ago, now that I was looking back on it.

"Did Brandy actually model for your costume?" I asked. Jay nodded.

"Mom helped me paint the spots on and touched up the dog mask." He turned it around in his hands. "Pretty good likeness, isn't it?"

"You'd recognize him anywhere."

Katy must have taken Brandy over to Jay's for a sitting. Maybe she had even ridden one of the horses or walked along the lane between the orange trees. I didn't know why the image of the lane and the horses and the water oaks should stand out so clearly in my mind. Probably it was the contrast of the Weary Why, all darting lights, electronic sound, and activated people, set off against the quietness and mystery of the darkness and the unseen house and lake hidden at the end of the little lane. That was silly, though. In daylight there was probably nothing the least bit unusual about any of it.

"Katy and I took Brandy trick-or-treating one Halloween," I said. "He was a great sensation."

"Wearing a man mask, no doubt," said Jay.

I giggled.

"He went as himself, and he got more treats than anybody else. One woman even cooked him a hamburger."

Katy and I had always gone out together on Halloween until the last three or four years when we had decided we were too old. Even then, we sometimes took the neighborhood children around, standing in the shadows while they collected their candy and apples and cookies. Naturally Brandy always went along, a sort of identification tag, so that people, looking out, would call, "Hi, Katy," or "Hello, Cammy." It was all part of another life, younger and simpler, nice to remember but impossible to return to.

Come to think about it, I couldn't remember hearing anybody in Gogi's Gang ever saying, "Remember?" or, "We always used to—" or, "When I was little—" In their company, I didn't say those things either, although I could have, and I was sure they could have, too, if they hadn't felt they were too worldly now for childhood memories.

"We better go in." Jay picked up his dog mask. "They'll be judging the costumes any minute."

"Oh, I don't think I—" Hadn't Gogi made some scornful remark about winning prizes?

"You'll win." Jay urged me inside. "No contest."

"You, too. I don't see any other St. Bernards in the running."

I put on my own mask and took a careful look at Gogi's Gang as Jay and I stepped back into the gym. Still no Eddie. So all right. If he couldn't manage to get here when he said—it was a quarter to eleven now—I could get along just fine without him. At least I could get along just fine as long as Jay stuck with me. Probably, though, he was anxious to get back to Katy, who must surely be through taking tickets by now.

"Katy'll be looking for you," I said. "Wouldn't you rather—"

He merely swept me into the grand march of costumed dancers passing the judges' rostrum, a crowd of clowns, princesses, hula girls, Walt Disney characters, even a couple of bearded, bead-hung hippies.

"Everybody march around again," the Student Council president yelled into the microphone.

This time the judges beckoned a dozen contestants to the rostrum, among them Jay and me.

"See?" said Jay. "I told you."

"Well, I told *you*, too," I said.

When it was all over, I had won the prize for the most unusual costume (girls' division) and Jay for the funniest among the boys, for which we and the rest of the winners received fun prizes—animal balloons, yard-long pencils, huge all-week suckers, toy musical instruments.

A hand grasped my arm as we left the stage and the Devil's Own started in again.

"Where were *you?*" Eddie, red-faced and in his usual clothes, elaborately ignored Jay.

"Well, you weren't here," I stammered, "and I couldn't just sit, and then Jay came and—"

At the Weary Why I was always perfectly satisfied with

just sitting, but I had to offer some excuse to Eddie. Besides, I really had been tired of staring at other people cavorting around the dance floor.

"We're leaving," said Eddie. "Gogi says—"

"But you just came!"

"Look, Cammy," Jay put in, "if you don't want to leave yet, I could—"

"Watch it!" Eddie snapped. "Whose date is she?"

"Just what I've been wondering all evening." Jay's voice was thoughtful.

Oh, this was terrible! That is, it was and it wasn't. If this argument came to blows and the boys got thrown out, the whole school would be talking Monday about how Eddie Arden and Jay Vernon had fought over Cammy Chase at the Halloween dance. On the other hand, nobody had ever battled over me before, so I couldn't help feeling excited and flattered.

"Well, if Gogi is going on somewhere else—" I laid a soothing hand on Eddie's arm, but I tossed a grateful look at Jay. "Thank you," I murmured, "for everything."

They gave each other parting stares, and Eddie steered me through the crowd and back to Gogi's table. I couldn't decide what to say next, so I didn't say anything. I would let Eddie do the talking, which he immediately began to do.

"I never thought you'd run out on me," he said.

I put on a disinterested air.

"How could I? You weren't even there to *be* run out on."

"I couldn't get out. I told you." His voice rose. "The old man made me stick around at the base reception to say 'Yes, sir' to all the brass."

"Lucky you!" I said—and meant it.

At least his father was interested, while mine— But why

replay that old record? My father didn't give me enough attention, and Mr. D. gave me too much—of a strictly instructional type, naturally.

"Whee," said Gogi, deadpan, as we pushed through the crowd to the table. "The prize winner." Her gaze roved over the dance floor. "Who's that with Katy Becker? Nils Larsen, I do believe."

Seeing it, I believed it, too, although just barely. Nils Larsen, the captain of the football team, was a blond dreamboat who had every girl in school goggle-eyed—except Gogi's Gang, naturally. They looked at everybody with the same cool gaze, even the Big Men in school, of whom Nils Larsen was definitely one, what with football and a long list of other activities. He didn't date much, and the fact that he was dancing with Katy wasn't necessarily a sign that he had brought her to the party. All in all, I was thoroughly confused. I had taken it for granted that Jay was Katy's date, and now I didn't know what to think—no affair of mine, anyway.

I sat down, hoping Gogi would change her mind about leaving. It was so great to be sitting here, secure among my friends and envied by everybody else who hadn't made it. I frowned. Jay didn't envy me, though, or so he had said—and I believed him. "There's more than one kind of jealous—" I studied his words. "Jealous" could be a lot different from "envious." It almost sounded as though Jay were jealous of Eddie on account of me, but that was ridiculous. Jay had never even asked me for a date, and when we were thrown together for one reason or another, he never made any effort to please me but was always sniping at me and my friends. I took my eyes off Katy and Nils long enough to glance at Gogi, who was talking to Joellen.

"We could go trick-or-treating," said Gogi.

Trick-or-treating when she had thought a Halloween dance was so unsophisticated!

"Where?" asked Joellen.

Gogi smiled faintly.

"Over at the Everything Shop?" she wondered. "Yes, that'd be good."

The Everything Shop, just across the street from the school, was a combination snack bar, drugstore, and five-and-dime, where a person could buy sandwiches, colas, coffee, aspirin, cosmetics, candy, notebook paper, and ballpoint pens. It was always crowded with people from Citrus High, eating and talking and making dates and sometimes doing a little last-minute studying in one of the back booths.

"Let's go." Gogi got to her feet and all the rest of us did, too. I cast a lingering glance at the dance floor, writhing with people. Katy was still dancing with Nils Larsen, but Jay had disappeared entirely. Eddie, tight-lipped, followed at my heels.

"Masks on, everybody!" Gogi ordered as we streamed across the street—ghosts, clowns, pirates, one spacewoman, and Eddie in his usual turtleneck shirt, with narrow pants and a sports jacket, just as he had come from the party at the base.

"Sharp!" I said, aiming to please.

"Oh, it's a groovy costume." His voice shook. "Disguised as a chip off the old block. Even my best friends wouldn't recognize me."

What kind of fight had he had with his father this time? Whatever it was, it had left him in a dreary mood, which my dancing with Jay hadn't improved any.

"You look great, anyway," I said feebly.

"Yeah." His voice was bitter.

"Eddie," I began. "I'm—"

I didn't even finish the sentence. I was sorry he was cross with me, but I couldn't truthfully say I was sorry I had danced with Jay. It wasn't a lot of fun being the only one in the whole group without a for-sure date, especially in front of the whole school. Eddie was worth waiting for, of course, but I didn't have to positively pine until he came, did I?

"What we do," said Gogi, gathering us all into a cluster in front of the Everything Shop, "is, we go in and yell, 'Trick or treat!' and see what happens. If the man doesn't come through with anything, we'll order something to eat and re-group." Her voice was gleeful behind her baby mask. "We'll be able to think of something."

A lot of other people from the dance must have had more or less the same idea about the Everything Shop because the place was jammed as we stepped inside. Our call of "Trick or treat!" was almost drowned out in the babble of voices and the sound of the jukebox playing loud music. Mr. Santos, the burly proprietor, was behind the counter with a white apron tied around his waist helping his wife and the waitress fix sandwiches and sodas and shakes. He cast us a harried glance.

"You kidding?" he demanded. "No treats—and no tricks, see?" He stood arms akimbo. "Aside from that what'll it be?"

I looked at Gogi who only said calmly, "Chocolate shake for me."

"OK, baby doll," said Mr. Santos. "You planning to eat with that mask on? We don't allow any anonymouses in here."

"Anonymice?" I wondered under my breath to Eddie, who didn't get it. I felt sure Jay would have, and Katy, too—not that it was the greatest joke ever heard.

"Oh, naturally." Gogi agreeably pushed back her mask. "All right, gang. The man wants to see what we look like. Cammy, grab that booth for us, will you? I want to see if I can find a toothbrush."

A toothbrush? What a time and a place to buy something like that, with the shop full of costumed kids over from the dance, but that was Gogi, doing what she pleased when she pleased. I dutifully sat down in the booth, said, "Sorry, this is taken," to several hopeful couples, and sat staring at some little flat boxes of flower-shaped soap stacked on the display counter alongside. I even reached over the side of the booth to lift down one of the boxes and sniff at the flowerets for a second—lily of the valley, as near as I could tell above the aroma of onion, ketchup, and grilled hamburgers.

"Darling soap." Gogi peered at me over the top of the counter. "Why don't you get some?"

I put the box back.

"Later maybe."

"Your order." Mr. Santos began unloading a huge tray. "Collect your crowd and sort the food out for yourselves, OK? Who gets the check?"

"Oh, the boys, naturally." Gogi waved a casual hand from across the soap counter. "Eddie maybe or Dwight or—" She and the rest came around from the sundries department and sat down in the booth. "Oh, Eddie, Cammy likes that soap. Why don't you—"

"I don't," I stammered. "I mean I do, only—"

I started on my cola, hoping that Eddie hadn't actually been listening. There weren't enough seats in the booth for everybody, even with Eddie huddled in the corner nearest the soap and four people jammed together on each side, so a couple of the boys ate standing up in the aisle.

"Let me out." Eddie polished off his sandwich and stood up. "Next shift can sit down."

Naturally, I had to slide out ahead of him. He worked his way through the throng, probably heading for the front door and some fresh air, but I was held up by a snarl of people in assorted costumes milling around the soda fountain trying to get waited on.

"Two hamburgers, one plain and one with everything. No, make it one with mustard and relish and one with tomato and mayonnaise," somebody called.

"Who gets the strawberry shake?" the waitress asked. "And the ham on rye?"

It was hopeless, so I just stood there while the crowd spilled over into the sundries department and pushed into the booths the minute there was a vacant seat. The cash register beside the door jangled constantly above the buzz of voices. A few people that I knew, unfamiliar in outlandish garb, nodded to me, and a girl from my history class said, "Love your costume!"

"We're leaving." Gogi and the rest, all except Eddie, who had disappeared in the crowd, began pushing their way in the general direction of the door.

Mr. Santos appeared at the register.

"I'll get it, Corinne," he told the cashier. "Ten of you, right? Who's got the check?" Everybody looked blank, and Mr. Santos scowled. "On a night like this, I gotta get a bunch that lose the check. OK, I'll figure it again. I got a real good memory. Three shakes, seven hamburgers, a coupla colas—"

"All right." Eddie appeared suddenly from the other side of the store. "I've got it." He laid the check down on the counter. "Seven seventy-eight, right?" He hauled out his billfold. "Out of ten."

Mr. Santos rang it up and counted the change into Eddie's hand.

"Seven seventy-eight, eight, and two makes ten."

We all began filing out, laughing and chattering. I waited until the last while Eddie stowed away his change.

"Hold it!" Mr. Santos darted around the cash register, plunged a hand into Eddie's jacket pocket, and pulled out one of the little boxes of fancy soap. "What about this, sonny?"

Nine ❖❖❖❖❖

I didn't know why Mr. Santos had to use that accusing tone. Naturally, Eddie had picked out the soap, probably for me, and then forgotten he had it, what with fighting his way through the crowd and getting out his wallet to pay the food check. But why didn't he say so? Instead, he just stood there without uttering a word, wearing his familiar closed-up expression that told absolutely nothing about what was going on inside. I hastily took the blame.

"My soap!" I cried. "For a—a birthday present. I forgot all about it." I took the box out of Mr. Santos's hands. "Eddie was just keeping it for me until—until we left." I dug my wallet out of my pocket. "How much is it, please?"

"One-fifty, plus tax." Mr. Santos gave me a suspicious look along with the change. "Sure you weren't going to forget permanent?"

"Of course not!" I said angrily. "I wouldn't do that." I searched for a way of establishing my honesty. "I—I'm Mr. Duncan's stepdaughter."

His face was blank for a minute, and then the light dawned.

"The principal, right? OK, then. That's good enough."
Nevertheless, he looked doubtfully at both of us. "Better
they should teach a memory course at that school maybe,"
he growled.

"Come *on!*" It was Gogi, impatient in the doorway. "Let's
go!"

Shaking, I wobbled out onto the sidewalk, with the soap
clutched in my hand.

"Gee, thanks," said Eddie. "I—" Surely now he would
offer some explanation, like, "A surprise for you, and then I
forgot." That wasn't what he said, though. "Who'd have
thought the old guy'd notice, with all that mob around? Boy,
did you save my life!"

His hand fumbled for mine as we followed Gogi and the
rest over toward the school parking lot, but I was too upset
to cooperate.

"Then you really meant to—" I began.

"Oh, Cammy, don't be so *wet!*" Gogi turned on me. "It
was tricks or treats, wasn't it? And what's-his-name didn't
come up with the treats, so he got the tricks." She gave me a
gleeful smile. "You and Eddie kept him so busy that the rest
of us got away safe." She hauled a fat candy bar out of her
pocket. Dwight had a pocket comb, and Sara and Joellen
had each picked up a plastic rain scarf—nothing that was
worth very much, from Gogi's standpoint, but still— "I
knew you'd come in handy, Cammy." She turned to Sara
and Joellen. "Didn't I always say so?"

"Cut out the needling!" Surprisingly, Eddie took offense
at what Gogi must surely have meant as a joking remark, although rather on the acid side. "She's a good kid."

"Naturally." Gogi's tone was light. "A good kid."

What was going on here? First Eddie had been cross at

me for dancing with Jay, and now he was mad at Gogi and defending me. My own feelings were beyond analysis, at least right then. Later, when I was back home, I would sort out my emotions. For now, I must manage a blank face. In fact, I didn't have to manage even that. I flipped down my mask, which I had pushed back while we ate, and again became a slightly green-faced spacewoman. Gogi stepped back to walk beside me for a second.

"You wouldn't go tattling to anybody about a little thing like that, would you?" she whispered. "Like telling Mr. Duncan?" Her voice died away almost to nothing. "I wouldn't, if I were you."

I shook my head. Mr. D. would be the last person I would dream of talking to about the trick-or-treat episode, especially since I had used his name to get myself out of a bad spot. I was a little ashamed of that. It would have been all right if Mr. D. and I had been terribly buddy-buddy like a real father and daughter, but we definitely weren't.

I knew I was blowing the whole thing up out of all proportion, anyway. A thousand kids must have been running around the town during Halloween playing tricks or treats and making off with *For Sale* signs and house numbers and all kinds of other things that were a lot more valuable than a candy bar and a couple of plastic rain scarves—and of course a box of fancy soap, still clutched in my hand. I pushed up my mask again and sniffed the aroma of the soap, strong enough to come through the lid. It didn't smell so great any more, for some reason.

"So now what?" I asked. "Back to the dance?"

At least nobody would be trick-or-treating there, except maybe for putting an occasional slug in the coke machine, but that went on all year long. Gogi yawned.

"We could go out to the Weary Why, I guess." Her voice was definitely unenthusiastic. "There isn't anybody good there tonight, though—just the Squares."

If Gogi had been Katy and the time a year ago, I would have said, "Come on over to my house then. We can fix sandwiches and dance to the record player." I could imagine how Gogi's Gang would react to that—the principal's house, records, not even a pool. It was too cool for a pool now, anyway, but it would be terrific to have one available as a status symbol.

"That reminds me," I said to Gogi. "I haven't brought back your bikini."

She gave me a long, level look.

"Bikini? What bikini?"

"That night when— At your house when we went swimming. A pink-and-white polka dot. Your mother said she—"

Her mother had said she wished Gogi had one like it, a puzzling remark, because my mother knew every item in my closet except, naturally, the bikini, which was still hidden behind my train case. Of course Gogi had said at the time that I could have the suit for a free gift, but I wouldn't dream of keeping it.

"I don't know a thing about it," Gogi said. "If you've got a pink-and-white bikini, you must have picked it up somewhere and forgotten. I do that lots of times."

Maybe she did, but I didn't, because I didn't buy enough clothes to forget about any of them. Besides, she *had* loaned me the pink-and-white bikini, no matter what she said.

"After all," said Joellen, "you did say you forgot about giving Eddie the soap to—uh—keep for you."

I realized that the girls were playing some kind of game with me, making believe that my memory was failing, but I couldn't figure out what the object was.

"You could ask your mother," said Sara. "She might remember."

"Oh, no, I wouldn't do that!" I said. "I wouldn't want her to even see it."

"Oh, I quite agree," said Gogi. "She might wonder, too, where you got it."

That wasn't the reason why I kept the bikini hidden from Mama. She didn't care for bikinis, anyway, and this one especially she wouldn't care for. I looked at the gang clustered around me—pirates, clowns, ghosts, Gogi in her little-girl costume, unreal people saying unreal things, like sinister figures in a nightmare. That was silly, though. These were my friends, playing some kind of trick on me, another of their offbeat jokes that didn't always make much sense as far as I was concerned. One of these days I would probably find out what it was all about. I glanced at my watch.

"I'll have to go home now," I said with dignity.

I really had a whole hour more, but that wasn't enough time for the Weary Why, in case Gogi finally decided to go there. Normally it would have been unthinkable for me to leave early and miss even a single minute with Eddie. Tonight, though, was different. I couldn't relax and enjoy myself until I had a chance to sort out all the things that had happened tonight and decide what I thought about them. I felt lost in a maze, with every turn leading to more confusion.

"Eddie, we'll be at the Weary Why after you drop Cammy," said Gogi.

Eddie nodded, saying neither yes nor no.

"Go with them now if you want to," I said sharply. "I can get a ride home."

Maybe I could, and maybe I couldn't. I could ask Jay to leave the dance long enough to take me home, but I wouldn't want to do that if he was Katy's date. There were always taxis, too, but I could imagine what a flap Mama would get into if I came riding home alone at midnight in a cab. If things got desperate, I could even call home and ask Mama or Mr. D. to come after me, making up some excuse about Eddie's having car trouble.

"A ride home with Jay Vernon?" Eddie snapped. "Just cool it. I'll take you."

And go on to the Weary Why afterward, no doubt, but I didn't even care. I said, "See you," to Gogi and the others and climbed into Eddie's car. What a spacewoman I had turned out to be, at ease nowhere, not even on earth! As we drove out of the parking lot, the music from the dance trailed behind us on the night air until Eddie drowned it out with the car radio.

"The soap was for you," he announced above the sound of "Purple Voices."

"I know," I said. "Thanks."

"For nothing." His voice was bitter. "I fouled it up good."

"Don't worry about it."

It was all I could think of to say to somebody who had been caught swiping something. Probably that was the wrong way to look at it, though. I must bear firmly in mind that this was all part of a Halloween prank, not to be taken seriously, or so Gogi said. I switched off all thought. In a few minutes I would be home and could sit up all night thinking, if I wanted to. Eddie pulled up in front of the house and just sat there with his arms dangling over the steering wheel.

"Are you OK?" I asked.

"I guess." His voice was sullen. "See you next Saturday?"

"Fine." He didn't usually ask for a date a whole week ahead, but maybe he was still fretting about Jay.

"You couldn't go out Friday, too?"

I shook my head. I was still strictly rationed as to dates. If this kept up, with all the studying, I would be the brain of Citrus High School. I was already getting A's on my papers, which wouldn't get me A's with Gogi's Gang but would at least let me out of the house a little more at the end of the six weeks. Even my term paper was progressing nicely. I might even finish it early if I could stop reading all the science fiction in sight and really get to writing. I had covered all the required references and commentary, but I kept looking up more and more novels, just for fun, besides haunting the newsstands for the latest science-fiction magazines. Some of them I passed on to Mr. D., who sometimes squeezed out a little time to take off into the galaxies with the space travelers.

"Restful," he said, "like detective stories. It's no more confused there than here."

I supposed he was thinking about the public schools, although I hadn't heard any more about people resigning, which was supposed to be a way of getting around the state no-strike law. Everybody was waiting to see what would happen at the special session of the legislature, according to Katy, who sometimes gave me a ride home in the afternoon. It was Jay, I supposed, who kept Katy informed about what was going on.

"Hey!" said Eddie. "Are you listening?"

"Sorry." I leaped back to what he had asked me the last time I had heard him say anything. "No, I can't go on Friday if I go on Saturday, or vice versa. You can take your pick."

"Saturday, then, for the Weary Why."

I sat there for a minute, with my hand on the door handle. Probably I owed him a few minutes more time, since I had insisted on being brought home early.

"Did you put in for college yet?" I asked, just to be saying something.

Maybe he would be going wherever Gogi and the rest were—a piece of information that I needed before I could make up my own mind. The logical thing, of course, would have been to ask Gogi herself, but I still hadn't had what I considered a good opportunity, because she was always talking about things that had nothing to do with education in any form.

"The old man decides," said Eddie. "I go where he says or he doesn't pay. Somewhere military, natch."

Another piece of the puzzle fell into place. I knew that Eddie and his father weren't exactly compatible, and now I knew one of the reasons. Parents! Why couldn't they understand how we felt about making our own decisions?

"Where would you want to go," I asked, "if you could pick?"

He shrugged.

"Haven't thought. Why should I?"

"It'd be fun," I said hesitantly, "if we could all go to the same place, Gogi and everybody."

"Could be." Apparently bored with the talk, he got out and came around to my side to hold the door, which he didn't always do if either of us was in a hurry. "Sorry about —things."

"Oh, but I had a good time. I really did." Not so much with Eddie as with Jay, and not because Jay had been especially agreeable either, but at least interesting. "And thank you very much."

"Cammy?" Mama called sleepily from the bedroom as I tiptoed down the hall. "You're home early."

I just wished she wouldn't stay awake to check on when I came in. I went straight to my room and shut the door before she could ask me why I had come home ahead of time and whether I had had a good time at the dance, which she had approved of strongly.

"I'm glad to see you going to the school things," she had said.

Probably she thought that was a tactful way of telling me that she wished I wouldn't go to the Weary Why so much— no news to me after all this time. I surveyed myself in the full-length mirror before I slid out of the spacewoman's outfit, which I still thought was a sharp-looking costume. I hung it in the closet and dropped my box of soap into the dresser drawer without even looking at it. Maybe I would give it to somebody for Christmas. I certainly didn't want it myself any more.

It landed alongside the slip from the Discount Center, where Eddie had bought his swim trunks. I picked it up and looked at it. Naturally, it still said $2.25, $2.25, total $4.50, plus tax. I frowned, suddenly remembering that the sack had had only the two shirts in it. I had opened it myself ripping out the staples that had held it closed until then. The swim trunks must have been in another sack except that Eddie had tossed only one on the back seat when he came out of the Discount Center. So where had the trunks been? In his shirt pocket? It wasn't big enough. Well then he must have been wearing them under his slacks, which meant—

I pushed the thought away, pretending it wasn't even there. It was just happenstance that I even had the sales slip in the first place so the thing to do was to pretend that I never had had it. It was absolutely none of my business where Eddie got his swim trunks, even if he had taken them from the Discount Store, as he had taken the box of soap from the Everything Shop. Surely there must be a reasonable explanation.

"I'm going straight from here to the pool," Eddie might have told the clerk in the men's department, "so I'll just pay for the trunks and wear them, OK?"

Unlikely, but possible. The horrible thing was that I would never know for sure because I couldn't come right out and ask Eddie. If he hadn't done it, he would never forgive me for asking. And if he had done it? Anybody who stole things would probably think nothing of lying about it, too.

"None of your business, none of your business," I chanted silently to myself as I lay in bed, curled around the hateful ache in my stomach that I always got when I was upset about something. Even when I finally did get to sleep, I dreamed wildly of witches screaming, "Clever, clever, clever," Eddie mumbling, "Well, after all it *is* Halloween," and a huge man brandishing a cutlass and yelling, "Who changed the numbers on those license plates?"

I woke up, heavy-eyed, so early that the morning birds were just beginning to chirp. If only there were somebody I could talk to!

"Katy," I might say, "I have a problem."

But what could I say then except that I thought Eddie took things—I could never think of him as a thief, exactly—and what should I do about it? But that was impossible! I simply couldn't humble my pride by running to Katy with problems that I had gotten into after I had dropped her for my glamorous new friends. Jay? Mama? Mr. D.? I shivered. What good would it do to talk, anyway? Whatever Eddie had done couldn't be changed now, and maybe, anyway, he hadn't really done anything except take the soap, which could be checked off as Halloween mischief, more or less on a par with the trash can caper. If I didn't like the way Eddie acted, I could just refuse to go out with him. And also give up the Weary Why, Gogi's Gang, and the sense of being firmly established among the "in" people? No, of course I couldn't. It was too ridiculous even to imagine. I would simply fill my mind with other things, leaving no room for the upsetting thoughts that were trying to push their way inside. Work, that was the thing, except, of course, when I was out with Eddie and Gogi's Gang at the Weary Why.

There as the days passed I again floated, cool and expressionless and detached, on a wave of music and light, with Eddie beside me. Strangely, I felt more secure in the gang now than I ever had before, completely accepted for some reason that I didn't try to understand. I hadn't forgotten how edgy Gogi and the rest had been after the episode at the Everything Shop, but now their whole attitude had changed.

"Not bad music," I would remark judiciously, and everybody in the gang would nod—a row of assenting parrots.

"See you around," I would say, departing, as aloof as Gogi had ever been, and there would be a little chorus of "Don't go!" or, "Want to shop tomorrow?"

"Sorry, but I'm still on curfew."

I didn't add that I would be in the clear soon because maybe I wouldn't be. If I did especially well with the grades, Mama and Mr. D. might expect me to keep the concentrated study up indefinitely.

"You don't need to knock yourself out," Mama said once as I staggered home as usual with an armload of books. "Roger thinks you're overdoing it."

"You wanted me to bring up my grades, didn't you?"

"Yes, but—"

Mama gave up and went away, frowning, but in the days that followed I sometimes caught her looking at me with a worried expression. I didn't know what she was worrying about. I wasn't worrying, or even thinking. When I was with Eddie and Gogi's Gang and most of the rest of the time, too, I simply turned off my thought processes and enjoyed the present without hashing over the past.

"Next week?" Eddie would ask as he left me every Saturday, and I would nod, sure of him at last. It was ironic that he should suddenly be catering to me just when I had doubts about him—or had had doubts, which I had firmly locked up in the farthest corner of my mind, where they couldn't possibly get out.

At the end of the six weeks, my grades went up as expected—all B's except for a C+ in phys. ed., which didn't really count from an intellectual standpoint.

"I knew you could do it," said Mama.

"You have a good mind," Mr. D. chimed in. "We're proud of you."

Naturally, good grades would be what he and Mama would be proud of instead of the fact that I was firmly established in the "in" crowd. That was the way parents were, interested in the less exciting things, although maybe to them good grades really were exciting. I had to admit that I was fascinated with the research I had been doing for my science-fiction paper—and not merely because it might get me a good grade.

Somehow, reading tales of what might or might not be going on in the galaxies opened up a lot of other possibilities, like our grapefruit tree branching out in all directions from the main trunk or a hallway leading into a dozen different rooms. This would be something I could have talked about to Katy if we had still been on the old familiar basis but not, naturally, to Gogi and Eddie, who seemed satisfied to skim the surface of the water instead of diving down into the depths.

"You may have two nights out a week now," Mama said, "as long as you keep your grades up."

"And not have to gallop home right after school every day?" I insisted.

Mama gave Mr. D. a questioning glance.

"I don't think that's an unreasonable request," he said.

"Well, thank you," I said coolly.

It was hard to feel grateful for getting back something I thought I should never have lost in the first place. Gradually, without actually telling anybody that the ground rules had changed, I drifted back to shopping with Gogi and Joellen once in a while after school, but not with the same interest. When I did go, I was careful not to pay too much attention to what they did. Instead, I strolled off to another part of the store, pretending to be looking for something else. I felt sure that Gogi, at least, realized that Eddie had taken the swim trunks; in fact, she had actually told him how clever he was. Of course she was entitled to her own views about things but I wanted to make sure that if she took a notion to do something of the sort herself, I wouldn't know anything about it. It was silly to imagine that she would, though, when she had plenty of money to buy whatever she wanted. Of course Eddie had plenty of money, too, or so I supposed, unless his father had clamped down on his allowance as a way of keeping him in line.

"What did you get?" Gogi would demand as we walked out of the store.

"Nothing much," I would say.

"Oh, we found some darling chains," Joellen would carol,

or "a sweet wallet" or "a new-type lipstick," which she would fish up out of the bottom of her tote bag, usually in a rumpled sack, with a reassuring sales slip attached.

In the routine of school, study, and the Weary Why, the days flew by, my doubts and suspicions lessened, and all the business about the swim trunks and the soap faded into the unreality of a dream, with the details, so sharp at first, getting pleasantly blurry around the edges. The reality was Eddie's hand warm on mine, the certainty of one or two dates a week, rock jangling through the air at the Weary Why, and the faces of my friends, relaxed and casual. Gogi even promised to get invitations to the Country Club Christmas dance for everybody in the gang.

"I'll like that," I told Eddie as he took me home one night late in November. "Formal, do you think?"

He nodded. "I guess." He drew a long breath as though it would have to last him for the next hour and a half. "The thing is, I won't be able to see you for a while. There's this girl—"

Ten ❖❖❖❖❖

"A—a girl?" I quavered after a long moment of silence in which Eddie seemed permanently bogged down.

"She's new at the base." The words came in a rush. "A—a colonel's daughter."

I felt as though I had been hit over the head with a rock. His words echoed in my mind: "I won't be able to see you for a while." What did "for a while" mean? Did he plan to come back to me after he got tired of this colonel's daughter or was "for a while" merely a way of softening the blow? He gave me a sidewise look and talked nervously on.

"The old man says I should take her out some on account of—" His father's idea, then? But why? What was the matter with me that his father, without even seeing me, thought I wasn't good enough for his son? Eddie's voice turned bitter. "Rank, see? The old man wants to wangle a cushy assignment next time."

Panic flooded over me.

"Next time? He's not—"

Eddie gave me an exasperated look.

"You don't think we *stay* anywhere, do you? The tour here's about up—new orders due any time."

I stared dully. Naturally, the colonel's daughter was bad news, but she might have been only temporary, in spite of Eddie's father. The other—the change of station—was an absolute catastrophe.

"But you can't just leave!" I stared at him in the dim light from the dashboard. "Your father'll have to let you stay with somebody—Dwight or Mac or Randy—until the end of school, anyway."

He looked at me as though I were crazy, and maybe I was —crazy at the thought of losing him.

"That'd be the day! The folks move, so I move. It's what happens."

"But don't you—" Oh, I wasn't playing it cool at all, not the way Gogi would have done, tossing it all aside as something of no importance. By then, though, I was beyond pretending. I blurted out what I really meant. "Don't you even care?"

He moved uneasily away from me and from the scene I was creating.

"Oh, sure. It's just that some stuff you can't buck."

"Oh." I got the message sharp and clear, like a knife stabbing me to the heart. "So that's how it is."

"Sorry about that." He hurried me up to the door, eager, no doubt, to get out of a sticky situation. "See you around."

Around where? I could feel a huge lump growing in my throat and tears coming to my eyes. I retrieved my pride at the last moment and managed what must have been the most insincere smile of all time.

"Thank you for everything," I said, "and have fun, hear?"

I fumbled blindly for the doorknob and managed to get

inside and down the hall to my room before I burst into the tears that I was sure Gogi would never have shed. I was still soggy with grief when I gave Gogi the news the next morning as we trotted down the hall to our last class—the news about Eddie's going, not about the colonel's daughter. That I couldn't bring myself to mention just then.

"So what?" Gogi shrugged, neither sorrowful nor even sympathetic. "People are always moving away. It's how things are."

It wasn't how things were for her. She had Dwight, who hadn't moved away and probably never would, since his father owned the biggest automobile agency in Valencia.

"Besides, Eddie hasn't gone yet," she said.

"I know, but—" In spite of myself, I started to blurt out the news of the colonel's daughter. "I won't be going out with him anyway. We—"

Gogi looked at me, sharp-eyed.

"You broke up? You don't mean it!"

I let it go at that, in spite of Gogi's obvious curiosity. Probably she couldn't fathom why I was so upset about Eddie's possible departure when I had broken up with him, anyway. Nobody else seemed any more understanding than Gogi, either. Mama, who must have been reading that book about how to talk to your children to show that you really understood their feelings, simply said, "I know you'll miss him." Probably underneath she was delighted because she had never been the least bit enthusiastic about Eddie. Mr. Duncan further enraged me by treating Eddie's leaving as a sociological phenomenon.

"This country has a shifting population" he said. "People just don't stay anywhere for long any more, especially the armed forces. Too bad."

"Too bad"—perfunctory sympathy, as though Eddie were

just a boy I had dated a few times instead of being the center of my entire life. Without him I might not even be a member of the gang any more. Mama must have gotten the same idea as she watched me moping around the house because she said, "Why don't you call Katy? You always used to have fun with her."

"Katy has her own friends," I said. "Besides, I have to finish my term paper."

I still planned to hand it in before Christmas and get it off my mind. Besides, I might rate a better grade by turning it in early—not that better grades were at the forefront of my thinking right then. But what was the use of thinking? As Gogi had said, Eddie hadn't left yet, but he might as well have, since I wouldn't be dating him, anyway. Maybe knowing he was here and going out with somebody else would be worse than having him gone for good. As it was, my grief returned every time I saw him in the cafeteria line or in the corridor between classes or zooming out of the parking lot. I didn't even care any more whether he had stolen the swim trunks and the soap. I only wanted him back and the situation exactly as it had been before, just as I had wanted everything to stay the way it had been before Mama married Mr. D.

"Better be doing your Christmas shopping" said Mama, a remark obviously meant to distract my mind.

"All right" I said irritably. "I'll get on it."

What a merry, merry Christmas this was going to be! Nevertheless, under Mama's urging I began making out my list: Mama, Mr. D., my father (sense of duty), Dina (ditto or less), Gogi, Joellen, Sara, Katy, I supposed, but what about Eddie? Under the circumstances, I thought not, although maybe I would buy him a record and have it ready in case, by some miracle, he appeared with something for me.

That I couldn't imagine, although he surprised me by telephoning one night.

"Cammy? Eddie."

As though I wouldn't know his voice any time, any place.

"Oh, hi."

My own voice was none too steady.

"Are you OK?"

"Absolutely."

At least I was breathing, although not with as much pleasure as usual.

"What's the gang been doing?"

I wanted to ask him what he was doing himself, besides taking out the colonel's daughter, but I restrained myself.

"Oh, the usual. Shopping and stuff."

"And the Weary Why, too?"

"I don't go there any more," I blurted.

How could he imagine that I would go back to the Weary Why, even though Gogi had invited me the very next day after I had broken the news about Eddie?

"See you Saturday," she had said. I gave her a questioning look. "At the Weary Why, naturally."

I had simply stared at her.

"Sara can pick you up. She doesn't have a date either."

"Well, maybe I—" But no, I simply couldn't. "I can't make it. Something I have to do with—with the family."

Like studying or clearing the table. Gogi just didn't understand that I could hardly bear even to think about the Weary Why, the symbol of all those weeks when everything had been a dream come true—Gogi and the gang, and Eddie there beside me, with his blond hair shining under the light.

"Cammy?"

Eddie's voice called me back from the trip that I hadn't taken to the Weary Why. He must have been saying something, which I hoped didn't require an answer. Maybe he was going to ask me for a date, after all. Surely he didn't have to spend all his spare moments with the colonel's daughter. Maybe, though, it would be better if he didn't ask me out at all, since it would only make it twice as hard to give him up all over again when his father got his new orders. Still, I knew I would snap at the chance for just one more date. I waited expectantly.

"I have to go," he said. "I'll be calling you."

So all right. He'd be calling me but obviously not to ask me for a date, so what was the point of telephoning at all? The only thing I had found out from the conversation was that he hadn't been taking the colonel's daughter to the Weary Why or he wouldn't have had to ask me whether I had been there. Maybe the Weary Why meant something as special to him as it did to me, something he didn't want to share with some other girl, especially one that his father had picked out for him.

That was another thing that I couldn't fathom. I couldn't imagine Jay, for instance, giving up his girl (Katy or anybody) just because a parent wanted him to date somebody else. Of course I had never met Eddie's father; maybe he was the juggernaut type that flattened everybody in his path. All Eddie did was to rebel vocally, unless maybe picking up things in stores was a kind of rebellion too, like tossing the trash cans around. Oh, I was the big psychologist, all right, busily understanding Eddie, now that he was practically out of my life!

"I thought you said Eddie Arden was moving away," Mama said the next day when she came in from grocery shopping. "I'm sure I saw him at the mall this afternoon."

"He's *going* to move away," I explained. "Not yet, but soon."

Mama looked at my tense face for a minute.

"Then why—" But she thought better of what she had been about to say and began putting the groceries away. "You might get the last sack out of the car for me, please. Oh, and there's what looks like an invitation for you on the hall table."

For the Country Club dance? I didn't know why Gogi wanted to waste an invitation on me when she knew I wasn't dating.

"Just ask anybody," she said later, as though it were the simplest thing in the world. "There are millions of boys around."

But not any that I knew well enough to ask to a dance, thanks to going around exclusively with Gogi's Gang for so long. Besides, anybody else would be a big comedown after Eddie and his smooth good looks. I felt the old gnawing ache that didn't go away but only grew worse as time went on.

"I wish you'd snap out of it," Gogi said in an exasperated voice. "Who wants you around when you act so stupid?"

"Stupid?"

"What's stupider than moping around just because you broke up with Eddie? We're all disgusted."

"But I—"

"There're lots of other people who'd be glad of a chance to get into the gang." Wounded to the heart, I simply stared at her as she issued what I recognized as an ultimatum. "Somebody'll pick you up for the Weary Why Saturday. Eight-thirty."

Somebody else who didn't have a date, of course, but nobody in Gogi's Gang ever minded a little thing like that. If *they* did it, whatever it was, it was the thing to do—a perfect attitude if you could persuade yourself in the first place. I shivered. Going to the Weary Why would be like visiting a graveyard, but if I didn't go, Gogi would surely drop me from the gang, and what else did I have left, with Eddie out of my life?

"All right," I said dully. "I'll be ready."

It was Joellen who came to pick me up, since Randy had gone away for the weekend with his parents. The difference was that Randy would be back and Eddie wouldn't.

"You won't be late?" Mama asked anxiously. "I don't like the idea of two girls out alone at night."

I didn't think she liked the idea of Joellen either, with her very mini mini-skirt and her heavy layer of eye shadow.

"It's on the expressway practically all the way," I said, "with lights and lots of people."

I didn't know why the anxiety. It wouldn't be the first time Joellen had picked me up, although usually Sara or one of the other girls was with her.

"Too bad about Eddie," Joellen remarked as we headed across town. "A real doll."

I managed to shrug.

"It's what happens," I said in a reasonable facsimile of Gogi's nonchalant air.

As we turned off the expressway for the Weary Why, I closed my eyes for a minute and wished I didn't have to open them again. I carefully looked neither to left nor to right until we had settled ourselves with the gang at the usual table. Without Eddie, everything should have looked different, but externally nothing at all had changed. The same bands of color streaked in restless motion across the walls, the same voices murmured above the jangle of the music, waves of cigarette smoke swirled around the lights, and from the stage the musicians still beat out "Cut 'Em Off at Generation Gap" and "Song of the Weary Why."

146

"The Ironical I's again," Gogi remarked in displeasure. "They always get them when nobody else can come."

I squinted through the dimness. Sure enough, there was Jay on the drums, exactly as he had been the first time I came to the Weary Why.

"I think they're great," I said perversely.

Let the gang hear my opinion, for a change. If they didn't like it—

"You just keep right on thinking so then," Gogi said with a little glance around at the others. "You've got a right."

Her air was so much as though she were humoring a difficult child that I felt hot color rising to my face. Why in the world had I come out here at all? "To keep my place in the gang," I promptly replied, a fast one with an answer, especially in these strictly mental conversations. The Ironical I's began on "Good-by Today, Good-by Tomorrow"—a number for every occasion, although it wasn't the band's fault that this one happened to strike an especially sensitive nerve. Jay was making a continuous little riffle with the drums as a background to the strumming of the guitars. I refused to meet his eye, if his eye was even looking for me. He was the last person I wanted to notice that I had arrived dateless.

"Good-by today, good-by tomorrow," the singer chanted. "Good-by for as long as I live—"

A little buzz spread around the table, but I was too busy trying to act cool to care what it was about. Gogi looked sidewise at me, and Joellen said, "So what? After all—" I turned as somebody arrived at a table for two halfway across the room. I was staring straight at Eddie, solicitously seating a girl with pale blond hair and a hot-pink dress. Turning a dull red, he half lifted a hand in greeting and then looked away.

The song went on:

*"Every hour is a longer good-by,
Every day is a longer sigh—"*

It was too much, it definitely was. I got up without a word
and pushed my way out among the crowded tables, through
the lobby, and on toward the cool dark beyond the parking
lot. I stumbled aimlessly along beside a hedge of Turk's cap,
but the music followed me like a persistent ghost.

"Good-by for as long as I live—"

How could Eddie have been so cruel as to come and throw
the colonel's daughter in my face? Maybe, though, it hadn't
been intentional. Hadn't he specifically asked me on the
telephone whether I still went to the Weary Why? I had
said I didn't, so he must have felt free to bring the colonel's
daughter there. What hurt the most was that I had been so
sure he thought of the Weary Why as our own special place,
just as I did—bitter proof of how wrong a person could be.

I roamed on over nearer the fence, where Jay's two horses
were standing, hypnotized, no doubt, by the sounds from the
Weary Why. I reached out to touch their velvety noses, but
they tossed their heads and darted away. I heard laughing
voices from a car in the parking lot and moved a little way
down the sandy lane that led off into darkness and eventually, I supposed, to Jay's house. He had said there was a
lake down there, too—not that a mere lake would be any
comfort to me. Even if it were the Atlantic Ocean, the waves
couldn't possibly roll in fast enough to calm me the way they
were supposed to do, according to all the poems we read at
school. "Roll on," etc., etc. Just the same, I took a hesitant
step farther into the protecting darkness. I simply could not
go back into the Weary Why and maybe run head on into
Eddie and the colonel's daughter. Probably I should have

had the courage to stay and face it out in the first place, with Gogi and the rest as protecting insulation, but it was too late now.

One thing I knew for sure was that I would never set foot inside the place again, Gogi or no Gogi. Tonight's visit had only made me feel worse than ever, even aside from seeing Eddie. I wanted to forget the whole thing, to get as far away as possible—out of Valencia, out of Florida, out into space even, if only the science-fiction books were real instead of imaginary. A new thought struck me. Maybe I could go and stay with my father in New York for the second semester. I had sense enough, though, to know that that was a really way-out idea. In the first place, he wouldn't invite me, and in the second place, I hadn't enjoyed myself when I had been there in the summer. I couldn't even get away from the pursuing music, much less all the way to New York. This time it was "Song of the Weary Why" that echoed across the parking lot.

"It isn't our world, no, no!
It isn't our thing, yeh, yeh!"

A truer word was never spoken. It hadn't been my world last summer when this all began, and it wasn't my world now. Somewhere, though, there must be one just right for me—an optimistic hope in which I had absolutely no confidence.

A slurred falsetto voice yelled, "Yoo hoo, honey!" as a car screeched into the parking lot, followed by the sob of a police siren, turned on low for just a second and then murmuring into silence. Somebody was going to get a ticket for something, I decided as I scurried a little farther down the lane. The horses trotted sociably beside me on their side of the fence for a little way before they veered off toward the deep pool of darkness under the big water oak—a perfect place for me, too, hidden from the clack of voices that was probably starting up at the Weary Why.

"He used to go with Cammy Chase," they would be saying, or, "I wonder when they broke up," or, "Did you see her walk out when he and his new date came in?"

I looked carefully at the fence. There wasn't room to crawl under, even if I hadn't been wearing my good clothes, and I couldn't climb over either because there was barbed wire on top. Maybe, though, if I tried close to one of the fence posts, I could make it without ruining my dress. I put my foot on the first strand of wire, steadied myself on the post, and started to climb.

"Hold it!" I lost my balance and slid awkwardly back down as tires whispered on the sand of the lane and car lights caught me in their glare. "Where're *you* going, Miss?"

The blue light on top of a patrol car winked at me, and a middle-aged officer gave me a discouraged look from the window.

"Well, I—" I gestured helplessly. "I was just—" My voice died into stammering silence.

"No place for a girl alone—and at night yet. Best if we take you home. What parents're thinking of to turn girls loose to—"

"Oh, no!" I could picture Mama's face if I came home in a patrol car. "Please! I'll be fine. I—"

"It's home for you," the officer decided. He got out and opened the door to the back, barred off from the front by heavy wire. "Get in, now!" I looked around wildly, but he nudged me forward. "Take it easy, Miss. You'll be OK. Just give us your address now."

Eleven ❖❖❖❖❖

"Cammy!" Jay came tearing down the lane. "What's the trouble?"

"Oh, Jay," I wailed, "don't let them—"

"This your girl? There was a note of reproach in the older officer's voice.

"Yes. Sure." Jay gave me a warning look.

"How come you let her go wandering around alone then? No telling what might—"

"I know, sir." Jay sounded as contrite as though he understood what was going on. "The signals got crossed." He jerked his thumb toward the darkness at the end of the lane. "I live just down there, and—" Improvising, he wagged his head at me. "You shouldn't have started out alone, though."

"You folks were up at the Weary Why, right?"

"Yes, sir." Jay took my arm. "Well, let's go." He nodded to the officers. "Lucky you came along."

He hurried me down the lane, while the patrol car backed out toward the Weary Why again.

"Oh, Jay, I was so scared!" I clung to his arm. "They were going to take me home in that horrible police car, when I was only— Well, I was climbing the fence."

"The fence? What for?"

"To—" To hide, of course, but I couldn't say that. "Well, the horses were over there under the tree and—"

He threw up his hands.

"You must have holes in your head! Listen, a lot of weirdies hang out around the Why. That's why the cops are always on the prowl." He turned to peer back over his shoulder. "They're gone. Now you can—"

"Oh, I can't go back to the Weary Why," I said. "I just can't."

"Well, I have to. The guys are covering for me so I could come and see if you were OK." A sudden idea struck him. "I could take you down to our house, the way I said, and then run you home after the Why closes. All right?"

"I came with Joellen," I said, "but—"

"I'll pass her the word—say you're not feeling so great." That was the absolute truth. I was still shaking from my encounter with the cops and from the shock of actually seeing Eddie with the colonel's daughter—so much worse than only imagining them together. "I'll tell her I've gotten you a ride home."

"Yes, fine, but what'll we tell your mother?"

"Just say you're going to stay with her until I can take you home. Mom's not the nosy type."

She definitely was not because all she said as Jay deposited me in the living room and left at a run for the Weary Why was, "How nice! You can help me with these letters if you want to. Shall I get you a cola?"

"Yes, please." I felt sheltered and at ease in this rather shabby living room, with books and magazines everywhere, a typewriter set up on a little table, and a big grand piano strewn with music. "May I use the telephone?"

"In the hall."

While she was out rattling ice cubes in the refrigerator, I telephoned Mama to say that Jay wanted to bring me home. "But pretty late. He's playing in the band tonight, so he has to stay to the end."

"Perfectly all right," said Mama. "Glad you're having fun. And thanks for calling."

"Oh, yes," I said. "Yes, indeed. Am I having fun!"

She thought I was still at the Weary Why, so at least I would be spared any explanations about how I happened to be here instead. Just how un-nosy was Mrs. Vernon, though? Might she casually say something to Mr. D. on Monday, like, "So nice to have Cammy with me Saturday night"?

"Would you just as soon not mention my being here?" I asked as I sipped my soft drink. "To anybody? You see, my —my plans changed."

She nodded as though she understood, although of course she couldn't possibly.

"I won't breathe a word," she said. "Now if you'll just take a look at these letters—"

It turned out that she was writing to all the legislators of the county urging them to support an adequate education package during the special session in late January.

"I don't want to send the very same letter to all of them." Mrs. Vernon pushed a stray wisp of hair back from her forehead. "In the spring, some of them voted for some good bills that didn't make it, so the idea is to thank those people and hope they'll keep on trying, and get across to the others that the public expects better things from them." She passed me a scribbled sheet of paper. "This is for the good guys."

She seemed to take my interest so much for granted that

I didn't have the heart to hint that I couldn't care less how the legislators voted. I obediently reached for the letter. After all, I had to fill the time some way until Jay came back.

"Do you think I'm getting the message across?" she asked, just as though it really mattered to her what I thought. "About why we just have to have more money for the schools, with the state growing the way it is? People won't want to move down here unless they think their children can get a good education."

"Sounds fine to me," I said, skimming over the page.

"Jay says I should talk tougher, but I always think you catch more flies with honey than vinegar." She smiled. "I don't know whether that works with politicians, though." She shuffled through some more papers. "Can you type?"

"Themes, mostly."

"I'm not so great at it myself—strictly hunt and peck, so I wonder if you'd mind—"

She lifted questioning eyebrows at me.

"Of course. Glad to." What else could I say under the circumstances?

"Such a help." She pawed around in the rest of her papers. "Then I can get the other letters ready. That one you have goes to—Yes, to Mr. Theodore Boehm. Here's the list of names and addresses."

I wondered what Mama and Mr. D. would think if I ever told them that I had spent practically the whole evening writing letters about the school situation for Mrs. Vernon. I was enjoying it, too, rather to my surprise, with Mrs. Vernon acting as though she really valued my opinion about whether to say, "I urge you to—" or, "May I depend on you to—"

"We're so lucky to have a principal who is in sympathy," Mrs. Vernon went on. "Some of the others don't think we should raise any fuss, but I don't believe teachers should just sit meekly and take whatever the legislature feels like dishing out, as though we were slaves, do you?"

"Well, no," I muttered.

"All we're asking are decent working conditions and small enough classes so we can give the students some personal attention and enough pay so we don't have to moonlight when we should be correcting papers. No wonder there's a teachers' shortage. They can get more money doing practically anything else."

I was only half listening, but I kept typing steadily, although not very fast. I hadn't heard much about the teachers' unrest just lately, and I was surprised that there was still this much excitement.

"Surely the legislature will come up with something," I said, trying to sound at least somewhat informed.

"Something, but what?" Mrs. Vernon said darkly. "The last bill they passed got chopped to bits." She abruptly changed the subject. "How about a sandwich?"

"No, thanks," I said. "I'm not hungry. Look, you don't need to sit up with me until Jay comes. I can read or something."

"Oh, I always stay up late. Besides, it's nice to have somebody to talk to when Jay's working." She handed over another letter for me to start on. "Do you have your college picked out yet?"

I shook my head. I was too upset about Eddie to care whether I even went to college.

"Jay'll be in junior college here for the first two years. That way he can handle a few jobs on the side and save up for the final two years—more if he decides to go into medicine."

I didn't think that junior college sounded as exciting as

somewhere away—not that I actually knew much about it. It had never occurred to me how lucky I was that Mama and Mr. D. were able to finance me in an out-of-town school —if they were still able to when the time came. What would happen if the teachers actually did walk out and Mr. D. missed a lot of paychecks while the thing was being settled? I had never worried about that before, and I wasn't really worrying now, just wondering.

I had finished ten letters by the time Jay arrived, ready to take me home, and I knew all the arguments that Mrs. Vernon was using on the various legislators.

"I can't thank you enough," she said as Jay ushered me out. "I'd probably still be erasing the mistakes on the first letter."

"It was fun," I said, "and thank you for letting me stay."

At least it had passed the time, even though it had been a million light years removed from what I had grown to think of as fun—the Weary Why, the evenings with Gogi's Gang, Eddie at my elbow. Eddie— I turned on an unnaturally bright smile for Jay's benefit.

"Shall we go?" I asked. "The folks tend to fret."

Probably they weren't fretting tonight, though, knowing that Jay, the reliable, was bringing me home.

"Back right away," Jay told his mother.

"No rush." Mrs. Vernon yawned. "I'm going to bed pretty soon, anyway."

"I'm sorry you have to bother," I told Jay as we trundled away in his car, which wasn't new enough to be impressive nor old enough to be a conversation piece.

"No bother." I glanced at his rather craggy profile in the dim light from the dash. It was strange to be riding around with any boy except Eddie after all these weeks. "I gave Joellen the word."

"What did she say?"

"Nothing. She bore up well, though, as far as I could tell. A pack of wooden faces, the whole—" He let that sentence die. "Sorry. I'm speaking of those you love."

He was, but he was right, too. Gogi's Gang were all singularly expressionless. Hadn't I tormented myself a hundred times, worrying about what they might really be thinking behind their air of aloofness?

"I shouldn't have run out, I guess," I blurted, "but I just couldn't stay, when—"

"You should have stayed and spit in everybody's eye," Jay growled. "Where's your backbone? Do you have to fold every time you see this guy?"

"Rah, rah, team," I said wearily. "Spare me the pep talk." Jay was another one who just didn't understand. "Haven't you ever been absolutely crazy about anybody?"

"Not that crazy," Jay muttered, "but yes, I have loved and lost, just like the TV shows."

I gave him a suspicious look. Was he just hamming it up for my benefit? But his face looked too grim for that.

"Well, I'm sorry," I said.

"Stiff upper lip and all that." He *was* laying it on a little thick. "One must be brave."

It must be Katy he was carrying on about, unless he was making the whole thing up to make me feel I wasn't the only person around who had trouble. Still, Jay had never seemed the type for make-believe, and Katy *had* been dancing with Nils Larsen at the Halloween party, although that didn't necessarily prove anything. It was a puzzlement but one that I couldn't care less about right then. If Jay and I were both miserable, though— I obeyed a sudden impulse.

"I have an invitation to the Country Club dance the night after Christmas," I said. "Want to go? I mean, if you don't have anything else to— Or if nobody would mind if you— I have to go with someb—"

Jay's lips twitched.

"You fell over your own feet getting that out, chum," he said. "Nevertheless, I accept your enthusiastic bid."

"Well, I just thought since we were both— And you said I ought not to just collapse."

"How true! We'll both go and sneer at—uh—everybody."

I felt a flutter of panic.

"Oh, you don't think Eddie'd come there, do you?"

"How do I know? And what if he does?"

"Well, nothing, I guess, only—"

"Only you fight back like an anemic mouse." He drove for a moment in silence. "All right! Want to withdraw the invitation?"

I did, rather, now that I thought it over, but Jay had been nice to me in his own outspoken way, rather like a brother pointing out the flaws in his sister's personality.

"Of course not," I said. "We'll have fun."

I doubted that, too, but I was in a mood right then to doubt the possibility of any form of happiness. All the same, it was hard to stay completely gloomy as Christmas came nearer and nearer. Silver trees glittered on all the light standards in Orange Plaza, loudspeakers filled the air with Christmas carols, the jewelry shops put all their best diamonds on sparkling display, the delicious scent of expensive perfume hung on the air in the mall, and the toy departments were crowded with mothers and fathers hovering over gorgeously costumed dolls and elaborate electric trains.

I didn't want to shop with Gogi and Joellen, who took more time than I could spare to wander from store to store and then go back to the first one again. Instead, I scurried around alone, bringing my purchases home to a room filled with Christmas boxes, rolls of bright holiday paper, and coils of shiny ribbon. After school, between bouts of typing my science-fiction theme, I helped Mama and Mr. D. drape colored lights along the eaves of the house and on the arborvitae bush beside the front door.

"We'll get out the Christmas decorations the minute school's out," said Mama, "so we can all work on the tree together."

Busy proofreading my theme, I didn't bother to answer. Probably from her standpoint this was a very special Christmas—the first since she married Mr. D.

"I'll hand in my paper tomorrow," I said.

The teacher, obviously astonished, said, "An early one! What a help!"

"I wanted to get it out of the way," I said virtuously.

At least that had been my original idea, but since I had lost Eddie, I had kept working mainly to keep my mind off my unhappiness—not that I was succeeding very well. The ache was there whenever I thought about him, which was much too often.

I went mechanically through the business of unpacking the battered old Christmas angel, the strings of lights, and the familiar ornaments that I hoped Mama would never replace. I had never quite lost my childhood sense of wonder at the warmth and beauty of Christmas, with the carols and the candles and the joy, but this year there was an added poignancy that kept me forever on the verge of tears.

"I'm sorry, Cammy." Mr. D., on a stepladder, fastening the last string of lights on the tree, peered down at me one evening while Mama was in the kitchen fixing hot chocolate. "Life can be rough some days."

I only nodded dumbly. If he gave me the usual adult pitch about how this phase, too, would pass, I would positively scream. He didn't, though. He simply dug a clean white handkerchief out of his pocket and passed it down to me without comment.

On Christmas morning I opened my presents as though I were standing off at a distance watching somebody else do it—a coral velvet dress for the Country Club dance from Mama, a wallet from Gogi, a lipstick from Sara, another from Joellen, a sport watch with a wide red patent leather band from my father and Dina, a mod notebook cover with squiggles of bright blue, red, and yellow from Katy, and, from Mr. D., a subscription to *Galaxy,* a science-fiction magazine.

"Thank you" I said, and, Isn't that pretty," and, "I'll enjoy it," all very mannerly, the way Mama had taught me. Mama had probably spent more for the dress than she should have, and Mr. D. had thoughtfully tailored the magazine to my current enthusiasm in reading. As I put the watch back into its chic red-and-green striped box, I found a small white envelope tucked under the tissue-paper packing, with my name in Daddy's writing.

"Try on your dress, why don't you?" Mama asked. "I want to be sure it fits, so I'll have time to return it if I need to."

I took the envelope to my room and opened it there. A twenty-dollar bill was folded into a single sheet of note-paper.

"Dear Cammy," I read. "Please buy yourself something extra with this. I should probably write oftener, but there's not much to say. Anyway, it's better for you to build your life as part of the family there in Valencia than to try to adjust to two sets of parents. This is my sincere belief, painful though it is. I think of you. Love, Daddy."

Quick tears came to my eyes and almost dripped onto the

new velvet dress. Maybe my father really did have my best interests at heart, as he saw them, or maybe he was just making excuses. Probably I would never know for sure, but at least he had taken the trouble to express himself. What he didn't know was that I hadn't done so well at being part of the family here but was still floundering around, not really reconciled to Mr. D. Of course I had even less in common with Dina, so I was strictly nowhere as far as family was concerned.

"Just right, I'd say." Mama looked me over when I came out in the velvet dress, and Mr. D. gave an appreciative whistle. "The color's perfect."

Even Jay was impressed when he came to pick me up the next night, carrying a corsage of pale yellow rosebuds in a silver box. Gogi would probably have an orchid, much more her type—maybe one of the greenish ones with flecks of brown at its throat.

"Wow!" said Jay. "You look great!"

It was nice to be admired by somebody, even though it was only Jay, pining for somebody else just as I was pining for Eddie.

"Shall we go?" I said, determined to act as though I didn't have a care in the world.

The evening turned out better than I had expected. By a heroic effort, I managed to keep smiling when I saw Eddie and the colonel's daughter, in silver brocade this time, coming into the ballroom, and Jay, as far as I could tell, didn't even quiver when Katy and Nils Larsen arrived, just after Gogi's Gang. When Jay and I weren't dancing, we sat in silence with Gogi and the rest—after all, she had gotten me the invitation—but most of the time we were out on the floor swinging with everybody else.

To my surprise, Jay was a terrific dancer, catching every

change in the beat so that I had to concentrate on every step. Maybe being hypnotized was something like this, a falling away of everything except the throb of the music and the motion of the body. Even the pang that I felt whenever I saw Eddie's blond head across the dance floor was blurred as the music held me in its spell.

At intermission, Jay and I milled around the club lounge, where the refreshment tables were set up. Katy and Nils, carrying punch cups, drifted over to talk to us, we clustered briefly with Gogi's Gang, and Jay, who seemed to know half the people there, took me around to chat with his friends. I had only one really bad moment, when I practically bumped into Eddie on his way to get some punch for the colonel's daughter.

"Miss you," he said softly. "One of these days maybe I can—"

Maybe, maybe, what did maybe get me?

"Marvelous party, isn't it?" I answered in a determinedly cheery voice as Jay loomed up behind me.

Eddie pushed on through the crowd, and Jay patted my shoulder approvingly.

"You're doing fine," he said. "It isn't so rough, is it?"

I shook my head, but my heart was still thumping like a trip-hammer. Probably Jay's would be, too, if he had happened to land practically in Katy's arms. I tucked my hand into the curve of his elbow.

"I think the music's starting again," I said, eager to return to my hypnotic trance, with no room for any fruitless guesses about whether Eddie actually intended to come back to me eventually. Eventually, though, would be too late; by then he would be long gone to his father's new post.

"We're going to leave early and go out to the Weary Why," Gogi said as we went back into the ballroom. "We'll meet you there."

I shot an imploring look at Jay.

"Wish we could," he said blandly, "but we have other plans."

Gogi's eyes showed a flash of temper.

"We can get somebody else," she said in an overly sweet voice. "Maybe Eddie and—"

"Do that," Jay said nonchalantly. "See you around."

"And thanks for getting us the invitation," I said. "It's a great party."

Jay grinned down at me as we stepped out among the gyrating dancers again.

"That gal's used to pushing people around," he said. "I'm not so much for being pushed myself."

I shrugged. I was accustomed to doing pretty much whatever Gogi suggested because it was sure to be the "in" thing, but I positively could not go out to the Weary Why, no matter what. When Gogi and the gang had disappeared, I looked out of the corner of my eye to see whether Eddie and the colonel's daughter were gone, too, but it was hard to be sure in the dimness, cut only by colored floods flickering fitfully across the room.

Jay and I ended the evening sitting on stools at Hamburger Heaven with Katy and Nils Larsen. I was surprised that Jay would accept their suggestion that we join them, but maybe he was trying to show me that he could be imperturbable, too.

"Nice party," Katy said. "Last fling, too, sort of. I have to spend the rest of the vacation working on my senior theme."

"Mine's finished," said Jay, "so I'm going to figure what we can do about the teachers' fight with the legislature."

"Nothing," said Nils. "We don't vote."

"Cynical!" said Katy. "Our parents do."

"I've got news for you," said Nils. "Two-thirds of the

parents couldn't care less what kind of education their kids get. They just want them out from under their feet—baby-sitting service."

"You're probably right," said Jay, "but maybe the legislators don't know that. Maybe they think the whole population's fit to be tied."

"Fit to be tied for fear their taxes might go up," said Nils. "Even my folks—"

"The special session starts the last of January," said Jay. "There's still time to organize a letter campaign, writing as concerned students."

I sighed. I might have known that Jay couldn't stay off the educational crisis for long. I didn't know what was so critical about it right now. Probably the legislature would pass a new bill, and if they didn't, there wasn't anything a few students could do about it, anyway.

"I helped Mrs. Vernon write some letters," I said, just to keep in the swim.

Katy shot me a look of surprise.

"You did?"

Probably she thought that Jay and I were so friendly that I was practically one of the family—an extremely unlikely situation.

"She has some good arguments, in case you need any," I said.

"I'll call some people," Katy promised. "Maybe we could even do individual letters for kids to sign if they don't know enough about the situation to write their own." She immediately started organizing things. "How about your being responsible for Gogi's Gang?"

"Well, I—"

But Katy was already passing out chores to the others.

"Could you try the football team?" she asked Nils.

"Right."

"And I'll just ask everybody I can think of," said Jay. "It may not do any good, but we'll have to try."

Naturally I didn't say a word to Gogi about the letter campaign. It would have been wasted breath, even if I had been terribly gung-ho about the project, which I wasn't. I did help Katy write a few letters for other people to sign, though.

"What a great bunch of kids!" said Mr. D. when I told him about the letters. "And they say young people today are uncommitted!"

The legislature convened right after our semester exams. Mr. D., looking more disturbed every day, hung on the television as the sessions dragged on and on, ending in a bill that pleased no one, according to Jay, whose mother seemed to understand all the ins and outs of the legislation.

"A $350,000,000 package," he said, "but the catch is that $136,000,000 of it is for noneducational purposes. So the teachers get blamed for a tax increase, even though the schools don't get even two-thirds of the proceeds. And the governor may veto even this bill."

"So what's going to happen?" I asked.

"Don't know—yet."

We found out soon enough when Mr. D. came home from school on Friday, haggard and worried.

"This is the moment of truth," he said. "The walkout's called for Monday."

Twelve ❖❖❖❖❖❖

An ambulance siren wailed its way into the driveway, and two uniformed men leaped out. I darted to the front door.

"What's the matter?" I cried. "What's happened?"

"You tell us," the driver said. "Where's the patient?"

"No patient," I said, weak with relief. "You must have the wrong address."

He consulted his clipboard.

"Duncan? 808 Willingham Circle?"

"That's right, but we didn't—"

Somewhere down the street a fire truck clanged nearer and nearer, turned at our corner, and screeched to a stop in front of the house.

"This where the fire is?" the driver yelled.

"No," I said. "Not here."

"Isn't this 808 Willingham Circle?"

"Yes, but there isn't any fire."

The ambulance driver and one of the firemen converged on me.

"Look, Sis, what's going on?"

I shook my head helplessly.

"Somebody's playing jokes," the ambulance man said, "only it isn't real funny."

I agreed. The mysterious grocery order that had arrived from practically the only store in Valencia that still made home deliveries, the large C.O.D. funeral wreath, the telephone calls that I answered only to hear heavy breathing on the other end of the line—none of them were funny in the least.

"I'm sorry," I said. "I guess I ought to call the police."

"Don't worry, we'll do it," the fireman said. "Turning in a false alarm's against the law."

A fuel oil truck pulled up, and the driver uncoiled a length of hose and dragged it across the lawn to the tank beside the house. He was back in a second.

"Tank's already full, miss. How come you sent for more oil?"

"I didn't," I quavered, "and neither did my folks."

I went inside and shut the door, leaving the three drivers to hold an indignant conference. Oh, I did wish Mr. D. would come home from the meeting where the teachers, who had walked out, were discussing reports from around the state! Or Mama—but she wouldn't be home until nearly six, now that she had gone back to work at the Clothes Rack until things were settled.

"Mrs. Smart has a place for me," she had insisted, "and this might last a long time."

"You're probably right," Mr. D. had agreed. "Things just haven't gone the way we expected. We thought it would be all over in a couple of days—schools closed to dramatize the teachers' problems, parents raising such a howl that the legislature would rush back into session again and come up with a really meaningful bill. All very simple."

That wasn't the way it had worked out, though. A lot of the teachers who had been going to walk out had changed their minds; parents were acting as substitute teachers to keep the schools open no matter whether the kids learned anything or not; school boards were blasting the teachers and threatening to accept their resignations and throw everybody out.

"Throw out thirty thousand teachers?" Mr. D. had said. "Ha!"

I couldn't help feeling sorry for him as he came in every afternoon from one of his interminable meetings, looking as though he were being torn in two. I would never forget the night he and Mama had sat for hours trying to decide what to do.

"Go with my teachers, who are risking their pay and their jobs to improve the school system?" His voice was hoarse with fatigue and worry. "Or stick in my office and try to keep the school running for the sake of the kids? How do you feel about it, Cammy?"

"Me?" Why should he ask me? "I don't know, I really don't. It's a—a problem."

His eyes, red-rimmed, gazed off into space.

"Maybe it's better for the kids to have a rough time for a little while now than to keep on for years with the same sorry old school conditions. It's not a clear choice—something undesirable no matter what I do."

Mama had laid her hand in his.

"Whatever you decide, Roger, we're right behind you all the way."

She didn't have any right to speak for me, but she gave me such a stern look that I mumbled a grudging, "Yes, naturally." I didn't know why I had to be dragged into their problems when I had plenty of my own. Naturally I was sorry that they were having troubles, but I couldn't think of anything I could do about them.

"I guess, then"—Mr. D. finally made his decision—"that I'll have to walk out with the rest. It would be hard to face them again if I let them carry the whole burden. I'll go back to school Monday morning long enough to leave instructions for the assistant principal. He can't afford to walk out; he has a wife in the hospital."

So that was what Mr. D. had done, staying only until noon on Monday to assign a motley assortment of substitutes to the teacherless rooms, according to instructions from the county. Then he had left his office and walked steadily across the parking lot to his car. I had watched him from my English room, and I had also watched the large group of students who had run out of their classes with hurriedly scrawled signs to cheer him on his way.

We're Behind You 100%, Fight for Better Schools and *Don't Take No for An Answer,* the signs read. I could see Jay, Katy, and Nils among the demonstrators, but I didn't make any move to join them and, naturally, neither did Gogi.

"Big deal," she muttered. "Why do they get so *excited?*"

That had all been nearly a week ago, and still the teachers were holding firm, but so were the legislature and the school boards. Rumors swept the school, which was in an uproar most of the time, with nobody learning much from the harassed substitutes, consistently heckled by the kids. In English class, for instance, Gogi would put up her hand.

"Would you please comment on the works of Dior?" she would say, all wide-eyed and sweet-voiced, or, "Do you consider Revlon superior to Max Factor in plot construction?"

Giggles all around the room, annoyance by the substitute, who usually said, "I suggest you look up your questions in the encyclopedia."

"Some of the subs aren't a bit bad," Jay admitted when I ran into him after school one day, "but some of them just aren't with it. You should see the mini-skirted number that's teaching our history class. She already made a date with one of the boys for the movies."

That was the way it had been all week, with the newspaper flooded with heated letters from people violently either for or against the walkout, the kids arguing and complaining in class, and the school board holding one special meeting after another. Katy was egging the Student Council on to put out a resolution of support for the teachers who had left, and Jay and a lot of others were under risk of suspension for organizing a mass meeting in the parking lot without permission. And now we were being persecuted at home by the ambulance, the fire truck, the fuel oil company, and all the unordered merchandise.

"Somebody doesn't love us," Mr. D. said when he finally came home to find me locked in the house, refusing to answer either the door or the telephone. "Well, nobody really thought this would be easy. The teachers are going to take a lot of punishment for a while. Idealists who try to implement their philosophy always do."

"But what'll I do?" I wailed.

It was all very well for him to carry on about idealism, but I was the one who had to cope with most of the devilment.

"Do just what you've been doing. Tell 'em we didn't order any of the stuff—fire trucks, groceries, whatever." His voice hardened. "Know what the state came up with today? Got an injunction forbidding the teachers to do anything to encourage the walkout—even talk. Every time anybody got up to speak at the meeting this afternoon, he got slapped with an injunction." He managed a weary grin. "It got almost funny. Everybody got into the act, trying to get an injunction for a souvenir. Free speech, my eye!"

"Grim," I said, and it probably was, but if he thought I was going to rush home from school every day to handle the rush of ambulances, he was absolutely wrong. Instead, I began shopping with Gogi and Joellen almost every afternoon, waiting to go home until I was sure Mr. D. would be there to take care of things.

As far as Gogi was concerned, the walkout might not even have existed except for an occasional "Everything groovy at your house?" to which I replied with an account of that day's assorted nuisances.

"I can hardly believe it," she would say with her air of indifference. "Who in the world would do such a thing?"

But there was a glitter in her eye, as though she thought the whole thing was pretty funny.

I didn't buy anything on our shopping trips because I had to count every penny, with only Mama's paycheck coming in, but just looking was better than staying at home to answer silent phone calls. As we went through the mall, I waved to Mama and Mrs. Smart on our way past the Clothes Rack.

"She's got somebody new in there," said Gogi.

"My mother," I said coldly. "She went back to work."

Of course Gogi's mother wouldn't dream of working anywhere except at home because she wouldn't have to.

"How nice!" said Joellen, who could say it because her mother worked, too, running her home cosmetic parties. "I'd go absolutely ape around all those groovy clothes."

"The Clothes Rack always handles good lines," said Gogi.

"Oakleigh Hill and Country Lass and— We'll have to shop in there again sometime."

I hoped she wouldn't. Mama had never liked Gogi, or Joellen either, and I was afraid her dislike would show through. I didn't want anything to happen to antagonize Gogi, who was practically my only escape hatch from all the turmoil at home and at school.

"I hear," said Gogi, "that Eddie's father isn't going to be transferred after all."

"Oh?"

I kept my voice carefully cool, but I felt a surge of hope. With more time in Valencia, Eddie might be able to spare some of it for me. He had said he missed me, hadn't he? My hope was diluted a little by the knowledge that he must have seen Gogi somewhere, maybe even at the Weary Why. How else would she know about his father's change in plans?

"You wouldn't be dating him anyway, I suppose?" There was a question mark in Gogi's voice. "Since you broke up."

I didn't even answer. Let her think what she pleased. If Eddie ever did ask me for a date again, she would see us at the Weary Why, which would be answer enough.

"Hey!" Jay called to me one morning in the school parking lot. "We're getting up a resolution of support, to be presented at the big teachers' mass meeting Sunday afternoon. We've got about eight hundred signatures here at school, and a bunch of us are going to take it to the rally—the president of the Student Council, representatives of the different clubs, and some of the football players. Copies to be sent to the governor, all the legislators from this county, the newspapers, radio, and TV. So how about your presenting it at the meeting on behalf of the student committee? Show you're backing your—Mr. Duncan—on the thing."

I stared at him in alarm.

"Oh, no! I couldn't possibly. I—I just—"

He gave me a long, chilly stare.

"I suppose," he said angrily, "your dear friends would think it was real square of you to stand up and be counted for once. Never say what you really think, look the other way no matter what happens, pretend you don't even know what's going on for fear you might lose your status with that crummy bunch of—" His voice shook. "All I've got to say is, you're not the girl I thought you were—or could be anyway if you'd be yourself instead of—"

He choked slightly on that last outburst, turned on his heel, and practically ran into the building.

I stared angrily after him. So that was the lecture for today—much the worst he had ever given me. I tried to shrug it off on the theory that everybody was terribly wrought up about the walkout, but I couldn't help feeling wounded. What right did Jay have to tell me what was wrong with how I acted? None at all, I told myself firmly, but that didn't make the hurt go away. I had thought that in spite of his frequent criticism Jay liked me, at least a little. Certainly he had been wonderful to me that awful night when the police had wanted to take me home in the patrol car, and at the Christmas dance we had had fun in a comradely sort of way.

"I don't care!" I muttered as I hurried on into school, where I knew the substitute English teacher would talk to us as though we were all eleven years old and had never read anything any more sophisticated than *Little Women*. She meant well, but really!

"I wouldn't care either about whatever it is," Gogi said behind me. "Things not going right?"

"Everything's great," I said, choosing not to mention the truckload of shrubbery that had arrived from one of the nurseries, plus a man who insisted that Mr. D. had telephoned an order for central air conditioning.

Luckily, Mr. D. had been at home both times to make the explanations that I was tired of making.

"I'll give our young friends credit for ingenuity, at least," he had said.

"*Young* friends? You think it's kids?"

"Oh, of course. Nobody else has time for this two-bit stuff. They'll get tired of all the monkey business one of these days."

"Who do you think it is?" I asked timidly.

"All I have is suspicions—strong suspicions—but I never judge anybody without the facts, so—" He smiled. "Are you learning anything at school?"

"Not much. The kids do a lot of heckling, so it's sort of chaotic."

"Just don't make it too rough for the substitutes. They're doing what they think is right, just the way the rest of us are. They can't see that we're fighting to get something for the schools, at considerable damage to ourselves."

"Yes, sir."

Only one good thing happened all week, and even that wasn't all good. As I was reading one of my science-fiction books after dinner, I heard shouting somewhere down the street—nothing to do with us, probably, but I was very jittery nowadays. I darted out to Mama and Mr. D., who were watching television in the living room.

"Somebody's coming," I whispered. "Hear them? Down the street."

Maybe it was a mob, coming to demonstrate, or— Sure enough, the sounds stopped in front of our house. Mr. D. got up and headed for the door.

"You girls stay here," he told Mama and me, "until I see what's up."

Outside I could hear the chant, "We want Duncan! We want Duncan!"

Mama listened tensely.

"You better call the police," she said. "I'm going out there," but just then Mr. D. called, "Marian! Cammy! Will you come outside? We have visitors."

We stepped out into a sea of familiar faces, interspersed with banners, placards, and a small combo of horns and drums playing the Citrus High School Fight Song. A cheerleader with a big C on her sweater stepped out in front of the crowd and yelled, "Let's hear it for Mr. Duncan!" followed by a long "Yeah, yeah, yeah!" I stood blinking in the glare of the yard lights. *Hurry Back,* one of the signs urged, *But Not Until You Win.* Another said, *We're With You, Man.* Jay and Katy were in the front row, with Brandy on a leash, wearing his own special placard, *Put the Bite on 'Em.* Katy smiled at me, but Jay kept his eyes on Mr. Duncan without even a glance at me. So all right, if that was how he felt. I did feel a little embarrassed standing there sharing in Mr. D.'s popularity when I hadn't done the first thing to deserve it.

There were a few more cheers, another burst of music, a "Thank you for your support; I can't tell you how much it means to me and my family," from Mr. D., and then the crowd began to disperse, swarming down the street to wherever the cars were parked. A police car nosed its way through the throng.

"What's going on here?" the officer inquired of the boys milling around the car.

"Nothing," somebody said. "Just a friendly little visit."

175

"That's right." Mr. D. came out to join the discussion. "No trouble at all. Quite the contrary."

"Somebody put in a call," the officer insisted. "Said there was a riot at this address."

Jay stepped up.

"A gesture of support," he said. "We're leaving now, anyway."

"You got a parade permit?"

Jay shook his head.

"This isn't a parade. We're just going home, like after a meeting. You wouldn't call that a parade, would you?"

"Go then," the officer said, "but leave us not hear of any disorderly conduct."

The patrol car spun around in the street just as Brandy, with his placard swinging, started ambling toward home.

"Brandy!" I screamed. "Oh, no!"

There was a thud as the car grazed his side and threw him onto the pavement. Jay, Katy, both policemen, and I reached him at the same moment.

"Whose dog?" the younger officer asked.

"M-mine," said Katy, with tears streaming down her face.

"We'll take him to the vet's," the cop said. "Wouldn't have had this happen for the world. All right, everybody. Out of the way."

I was crying, too, as Jay and Katy climbed into the back of the police car, with Brandy stretched out on the seat between them.

"Oh, how awful!" I wailed as Mama urged me into the house. "Do you think h-he's—"

"I hope not." Mama patted my shoulder.

"I'm furious," I said, "absolutely furious! It never would have happened if those big jokesters hadn't called the cops just to devil us. If I ever find out who—"

I tore into my room and lay crying on the bed until Mama tapped on my door.

"Katy called," she said. "Brandy's still alive—has some broken ribs and maybe some internal injuries. She'll call again when she knows more."

Mr. D. peered at me over her shoulder.

"Such a fine gesture from these kids," he said, "and then to have it end like that!" He looked even more harassed than usual. "It's frightening sometimes how little control we have over what happens. Start out on what looks like the right road, and half the time you end up in a muddy field somewhere."

I didn't want philosophy at the moment. I just wanted somebody to say, "Everything's going to be all right," even though maybe it wouldn't be. The next morning I angrily recounted the whole episode to Gogi, who merely said, "Too bad. I heard some of the kids were going out to your house."

But naturally she hadn't joined them. Still, she must have felt she ought to offer some consolation because she said, "Why don't you go shopping with me this afternoon? I'm looking for a skirt and a sweater and some other things."

Joellen came, too, muttering that she hadn't been able to find the right blouse to go with her new jumper.

"Let's try the Clothes Rack this time," Gogi suggested. "They might have some new things in."

I knew they did have because at breakfast, probably trying to take my mind off Brandy, Mama had babbled on about the new spring colors.

I hung back a little at the door of the Clothes Rack.

"All right, but—"

Still, I didn't know any way to keep Gogi and Joellen from shopping at the Clothes Rack if they wanted to. Maybe Mrs. Smart would wait on them so Mama wouldn't have to. Mrs. Smart was busy typing statements, though, when we came in, and Mama said, "Hello, girls. May I help you or are you just looking?"

"Both, actually," Gogi said in her most remote voice. "We just can't seem to find what we want, a skirt for me and a blouse for Joellen, to start with."

"I think we can show you something you'll like," said Mama, determinedly amiable. "Some especially nice junior things came in yesterday—just unpacked, in fact."

Mrs. Smart stuck her head out of the office and said, "Hi, Cammy! Aren't I the lucky one to get your mother back?"

I leaned on the counter talking to her while, in the dressing room, Gogi was saying to Mama, "So fascinating to work in a shop like this. I know I'd buy just everything for myself."

Mrs. Smart grinned as Mama, with a wry smile, came out to collect a second armload of clothes for Gogi and Joellen to try on.

"Cammy!" Gogi called. "Come in here a minute and see what you think about this." It was a ruffled blouse with full sleeves drawn into a tight band. "Is your comb in your tote bag? I forgot to bring mine. Oh, and run out and see if you can find the next size smaller in this blouse. This one could be the least bit too big."

I brought back the next size, picked up my tote bag, and went back out to Mrs. Smart.

"I believe I'll try this blue skirt," Gogi said as Mama took her whatever she had sent for, "but I'd like to see it in the other colors, too—gold and green—and Joellen wants to see this blouse in a gray. We just can't decide."

They still couldn't decide when they emerged from the dressing room a few minutes later.

"We'll think it over," Gogi said brightly, "and thank you

so, so much." She might as well have added "my good woman," which was exactly what her condescending tone conveyed. I looked at Mama's still face. "Come on, Cammy."

We were halfway out the door when Mama shot a look at Mrs. Smart, who nodded.

"I'm sorry, Cammy, that these are your friends," Mama said in a tight voice, "but I'll have to ask them to step inside again."

She rummaged in Joellen's tote bag and brought out a violet sweater, still folded in tissue paper. Mrs. Smart flipped up the hem of Gogi's dress to show two skirts that she was wearing underneath.

"Will you call the police, Marian?" Mrs. Smart said briskly. "I'm sick and tired of being stolen blind in this shop."

"Oh, don't be silly," said Gogi. "I'll give the stuff back. It's just a game, like—"

"Call the police," Mrs. Smart repeated.

"I wouldn't do that," Gogi said softly, "until you see what Cammy has in *her* tote bag."

Thirteen ❖❖❖❖❖❖

I stared unbelievingly at Gogi.

"Why, I w-wouldn't take anything! You know that!"

"No?" She turned to Mrs. Smart. "Just look in her tote bag, like I said."

"Of course." I laid it down on the counter. "You're welcome to look all you like. I wouldn't dream of—"

Before the words were even out of my mouth, I felt a horrible sinking sensation. I might not take anything, but I was sure Gogi wouldn't have any scruples whatsoever about planting something in my tote bag if it happened to suit her. It would be an easy way of getting a package out of the store and good insurance against having to take the rap all alone in case she got caught herself. I wasn't even surprised, then, when Mama dug into my tote bag and came up with a pair of linen shorts in a pale avocado shade.

"Oh, Cammy!" Mama's voice was a wail.

"I didn't put them there, no matter what she says! I truly didn't. I left my tote bag in there a minute because she wanted to borrow my comb, and she must have—"

"Some story!" Gogi's voice was completely nonchalant. "You wouldn't take anything?" She turned to Mama. "She has a bikini from Albin's at home in her closet right now."

"I don't believe it!" said Mama. "Cammy wouldn't—"

"Oh, I've got it, all right," I said, "but Gogi loaned it to me one night we were swimming at her house. Joellen remem—"

But I knew there was no use expecting any help from Joellen, who had played right along with Gogi at Halloween when they had all pretended not to know anything about the pink-and-white bikini. Not only that, Joellen would be sure to verify Gogi's story about my having taken the shorts. Eddie? The rest of the gang? Obviously they would back up Gogi, no matter what she said. I felt like an animal caught in a trap, darting frantically in every direction trying to get out but knowing all the time that there was no exit.

"I really don't see what all the fuss is about anyway," said Gogi. "Everybody takes little things, just for kicks—dues in the club and all that."

"My mother'll pay, if that's how you want it," Joellen chimed in. "It isn't as though you'd be out anything."

Mrs. Smart gave her a speculative glance.

"Suppose we telephone all the parents then," she said, "and see what they have to say. Then I'll decide whether to prosecute."

"I'll call Roger, too," said Mama.

Gogi shrugged.

"Suit yourselves, people," she said, "but I'd think over that bit about calling the cops." She gave Mama a cold stare. "My father is a real big shot around this town, and he could keep Mr. Duncan from ever getting his job back. He knows absolutely everybody on the board of education."

This time I really was horrified. Nobody had told me that the teachers who had walked out might actually lose their jobs. Hadn't Mr. D. said that the school boards couldn't accept thirty thousand resignations? Maybe, though, they could accept one if Mrs. Smart insisted on going to the police. When a principal's stepdaughter was branded as a shoplifter— And with Gogi's father probably burning with revenge because Mama was accusing his daughter— Oh, no, Mr. D. wouldn't have a chance, and it was mostly my fault.

"Oh, Mrs. Smart," I begged, "I wish you'd—"

"I've already agreed to discuss it," she snapped, "which is more than I ought to do." She turned to Gogi and Joellen. "If you girls really couldn't pay for the stuff, I might be a little more lenient, but you both have plenty of money, so what's the point?"

"You don't have to talk as though we were criminals, like with a gun," Gogi flared. "Just taking a few things is different. It's more of a—a game."

"Some game!" Mrs. Smart gestured toward the telephone. "Well, are you going to call your parents, or shall I?"

"You," said Gogi. "It's your idea, not mine."

I sat in miserable silence while Mrs. Smart tried to reach Gogi's mother at home. The telephone rang on and on.

"She's at a committee meeting," Gogi said helpfully. "She always is."

"Then I'll try your— Oh, hello. Mrs. Blakewood? This is Angie Smart at the Clothes Rack. I wonder if you could come down to the shop. We have a rather serious problem. Yes, I know, but— I would prefer not to discuss it on the telephone, but if you— And I suggest you bring your husband, too." She pushed the office door shut with her foot so we couldn't hear the rest of the conversation, but in a minute I heard her dialing again, probably to Joellen's mother. She opened the door. "It's all yours, Marian, if you want to call your husband."

Gogi and Joellen and I simply sat in stony silence, careful

not to look at each other. If I had opened my mouth, I would have burst into tears. Everything was so terribly clear to me now. Smart too late, I kept remembering little scraps of conversation that hadn't quite made sense at the time but now were bitterly revealing. "Oh, I have big plans for her" (the principal's naïve stepdaughter being used to make the game extra exciting). "I knew she'd come in handy" (as a diversionary action at the Everything Shop and probably a lot of other places, too). I recalled the mysterious extra record the first time I had ever gone shopping with Gogi and the others, the generous gifts of lipstick and mascara, the shopping expeditions with hardly anything ever actually bought but, I knew now, a lot of items shoplifted, like the bikini, either then or later.

"Oh, this is so stupid!" Gogi burst out.

Not half as stupid as little Cammy Chase, too dazzled by her apparent popularity with the "in" group to believe what should have been as plain as the nose on her face. The whys and wherefores didn't matter now, though—only the cold facts. I was in a holy mess, with my word against that of two other people who obviously intended to drag me into trouble along with themselves, in case they couldn't use me to get them out of their difficulties.

Especially galling was the fact that probably half the school had known all the time what Gogi's Gang had been up to. Even Jay, definitely not in any "in" group, had warned me about my new friends, although without making any specific accusations. And Katy? If Jay knew, probably she did, too.

"As soon as everybody gets here, I'm going to put the closed sign on the door," Mrs. Smart told Mama. "This isn't a big enough place so we can handle customers and arguments at the same time."

Mama, white-faced, only nodded.

"Your— Roger'll be right down." She added a not very convincing pat on my shoulder. Was it possible that even Mama didn't believe me?

"Mama," I said, "I really didn't—"

"I know. Don't talk about it now. Wait until— Oh, here comes somebody."

It was Joellen's mother, elegant in elaborate makeup (she sold the stuff, didn't she?) and what was probably a Pucci dress.

"Joellen," she said, "I just don't understand what's going on. You know I have a big cosmetic party to put on tonight, and I'll have to—"

Joellen glowered at her.

"Sorry about that. All you have to do is to—"

This time it was Mrs. Blakewood who came rushing in.

"Now, Gogi," she said, "whatever you've done, your father will get you out of it. I'm sure you didn't mean any harm."

Gogi shrugged.

"Talk to her." She pointed to Mrs. Smart. "She's the one that's making a big thing out of just a little fun and games."

Mrs. Smart didn't answer that. She only said, "When everybody's here, we'll begin—and no sooner. Due process."

Gogi's father arrived next.

"Now what's this all about?" he asked, a little on the blustery side but still obviously upset. "I'm sure we can work everything out somehow. First, Mrs. Smart, tell me your side of the story."

Mr. D., breathless, galloped in, and Mrs. Smart shut the door, locked it, and pulled the draperies across the display window.

"This is the situation," she began. "These girls came into my shop this afternoon and—"

At the end of her recital, there was a long silence and then a babble of parental voices. Mr. D.'s rose above all the rest.

"You say they all took things?" he asked. "All three?"

"I hesitate to believe it of Cammy," Mrs. Smart said, "but—"

"I didn't!" I cried for what seemed to be the twentieth time. "I never even saw those shorts before!"

"What *I* think," Joellen said airily, "is that Cammy sneaked that blouse into my tote bag. You can't prove she didn't."

"Or that she did either," said Mr. D.

"Blouse?" said Mrs. Smart. "Did you say blouse?"

Joellen turned scarlet.

"I mean s-sweater," she said. "A—a slip of the tongue."

"Just the same," said Mrs. Smart, "I'll take a look. Excuse me, folks."

She undid the top button of Joellen's blouse, under which was another one, pale gray voile with smoky pearl buttons.

"I suppose," said Mr. D., rising to battle, "that Cammy put that on you when you weren't looking, too." He turned to Mrs. Smart. "May I see the shorts that Cammy's friends claim she stole?"

"Certainly." Mrs. Smart handed them over, and Mr. D. inspected them carefully.

"M'm. Very pretty. What size?"

"I think—" Mrs. Smart put on her glasses and turned out the label. "Yes. Eleven."

"Hey!" I said. "I wear a nine."

"That's what I thought your mother said," Mr. D. said. "And I don't think you'd be stupid enough to take something that was the wrong size—a girl that gets B's in math."

"Gogi wears an eleven," I said.

"Then I'm sure, Mrs. Smart, you must agree that Cammy didn't take the shorts but had them planted on her," said Mr. D. with an air of summing up the case. "Naturally I couldn't believe she would steal anything, but I always like to prove things to everybody's satisfaction."

"Don't forget that bikini from Albin's," Gogi said sulenly.

"What bikini?" Mr. D. demanded.

"The one I didn't take!" I said. "Gogi loaned it to me, and now she's pretending she didn't."

Mr. D. turned on Gogi.

"I'm afraid, with the credibility gap you've just established, you'd have a rough time trying to pin anything else on my daughter. All right, Cammy. I guess we can go now." He turned to Mama. "Ready, Marian? I'm sure these people would rather discuss their problems in private."

Gogi jumped to her feet, glaring at Mr. D. and the circle of parents.

"You'll be sorry! If you let Mrs. Smart have us arrested, my father'll see you never hold a job around here again. He knows everybody in this town and—"

Mr. D. gave her a long look.

"That's the way it'll have to be, then," he said slowly. "The truth is the truth, and it can't be pushed around to suit my personal convenience or anybody else's." He turned to Mrs. Smart and the others. "I hope you folks can work out your problems satisfactorily. If I can help, feel free to ask."

"Oh, boy, are you noble!" Gogi sneered. "Wait until you're out on your ear and broke and—"

"That's enough, Gogi!" Her father's voice cracked like a whip. "I'm opposed to this teachers' walkout, but I'm not going to threaten a man's job—even if I could—for something that doesn't have anything to do with his abilities or his opinions either. Blackmail is the word for that."

"Oh, Gogi!" Mrs. Blakewood wailed. "What's everybody going to think? All our friends—"

"Tough," said Gogi. "My heart bleeds."

"Quiet!" Mr. Blakewood roared.

He and Mr. D. gravely shook hands, and we left—Mama and Mr. D. and I. I cast a backward look at Gogi and Joellen and received icy stares in return.

"Next time," Gogi said through her teeth, "I'll send the wreckers out to your house, too." She and Joellen exchanged defiant glances. "It was a howl while it lasted, though."

"Another thing off the agenda," Mr. D. drew a long, weary sigh as we headed for home. "Those bratty kids! In this case it's easy to see why, though—probably a subconscious bid for parental attention, which they hadn't had enough of. Too many busy parents tend to think cash is cheaper than time as far as their youngsters are concerned."

There spoke the educator, analyzing motives and reasons, but anybody who had laid his job on the line to defend me, the original Hostility Kid, was entitled to analyze things all day every day if he wanted to.

"I'm sorry," I said in a choked voice.

"Live and learn," he said, very matter of fact, but I knew he was reading my admiration loud and clear.

"Listen! A far-off drummer
Setting a measured beat—"

Katy and Nils Larsen and I were sitting at a table at the Weary Why while, onstage, Jay and the rest of the Ironical

I's, caught in the shifting colors of the spotlight, were crashing forth with "The Distant Drummer."

"A celebration," Jay had said on the telephone that morning. "I guess you know the teachers are going back to work Monday."

"So I hear."

With all the wisdom I had learned the hard way from Gogi's Gang, I wasn't surprised that the finish of the walkout wasn't a completely happy ending—lovers walking off into the sunset, the heroine untied from the railroad track just in time. In this case the drawback was that the teachers were having to accept an inadequate and unfair bill. On the other hand, they had pried loose more school funds than ever before.

"Nothing more we can do right now," Mr. D. had explained, "and the understanding is that all the teachers will be taken back, which is what we've been holding out for. I'm not sure that all the boards statewide will keep to that, but we're assured we're in the clear in this county."

Hence the celebration, although of a bittersweet type, for more reasons than one.

"The thing is," Jay had said, "I have to work at the Weary Why, but Nils and Katy would be glad to sit with you until I finish. It depends on how much you don't want to go there."

I thought it over briefly.

"I don't believe I'll mind too much," I said. "The spotlight has sort of shifted." Shifted from Eddie to Jay, from Gogi to Katy. "Besides—"

Besides, a lot of things looked different, now that I was out with the "in" gang and in with the action people, busily working on petitions, making posters, and helping conduct rallies on behalf of the teachers.

"Welcome back!" Katy had said when I had gone to her with my apologies for the way I had acted all these months.

"What a hang-up!" I bent over to avoid her eyes and to pat Brandy, who was convalescing from his accident. "It'd take most people years of practice to be that stupid!"

"Forget it! We all have our snafus." A pause. "I'm happy on account of Jay, too. He always thought you were so great."

Not always, but I could forget that, too, now that I was back on familiar ground again.

I looked warily around the Weary Why. The table where I had sat so many times with Eddie and Gogi's Gang (now off Mrs. Smart's hook and presumably under their parents' strict surveillance) was occupied by some young people I had never seen before. I waited for the expected wave of grief, but there was only a nostalgic ache, not so much for things as they had been as for what they might have been. I pulled back my thoughts once and for all to the music and Jay, to the future and the now.

> *"Listen! A far-off drummer*
> *Setting a measured beat,*
> *I step to that different drummer*
> *On eager, dancing feet."*

Jay, smiling straight at me as the music ended with a great thundering of drums, stood to take his bow with the rest of the Ironical I's and then came to join us for intermission.

"I like that song," I said, sliding my hand into his.

"So do I," he agreed, "being a drummer."

"A different drummer," I said gravely. "Better, too."